The Good Parts

The Good Parts

{ THE BEST EROTIC WRITING IN MODERN FICTION }

EDITED BY J. H. BLAIR

BERKLEY BOOKS, NEW YORK

THE GOOD PARTS

A Berkley Book / published by arrangement with
The Reference Works

PRINTING HISTORY
Berkley trade paperback edition / February 2000

A continuation of acknowledgments appears on pages 221–25.

The Penguin Putnam Inc. World Wide Web site address is
http://www.penguinputnam.com

ISBN: 0-425-17225-2

BERKLEY®
Berkley Books are published by The Berkley Publishing Group,
a division of Penguin Putnam Inc., 375 Hudson Street, New York, New York 10014.
BERKLEY and the "B" design
are trademarks belonging to Penguin Putnam Inc.

PRINTED IN THE UNITED STATES OF AMERICA

10 9 8 7 6 5 4 3 2 1

Contents

Contents

Contents

Contents

Contents

On Finding the Good Parts—
A Reader's Preface

WHEN I WAS TWELVE I LOVED TO RIDE THE SUBWAYS. ONE day during summer vacation, my friends Danny Franceschini, Mark Feingold, and I took the slow, sunny local out to Flushing and, after wandering around Main Street and Northern Boulevard, found ourselves in Gert's Department Store staring at five tables full of pulp paperbacks—"All Books: 3 for $1.00." We decided this was too good a deal to pass up. Since we would pass the books back and forth it would be like reading nine books for a buck. I remember that my three choices were *The Black Satin Jungle; Darling, This Is Death;* and *Tropic of Carla.* And either Danny or Mark bought one called *Kiss, Kiss, Kill Kill.* Later, our parents gave us the usual line that we shouldn't be spending our money on junk but they weren't really upset. And Mr. Feingold, who read everything from Balzac to Eric Ambler to Alan King's *Anyone Who Owns His Own Home Deserves It,* said, "Just remember to mark the pages with the good parts."

The summer of my sophomore year at Northwestern, I was dating a Sarah Lawrence girl from West 82nd Street named

Mindy. Sometimes we would sit on a hillside in Central Park with the smell of suntan butter and the barely audible radio sound of the Mets chasing the Cubs. She was reading *Couples*. I was reading *Portnoy's Complaint*. In between sips of iced tea Mindy would say, "Now this is good," and read aloud:

> *His blood brooded on Foxy; he dwelled endlessly upon the bits of her revealed to him—her delicate pubic fleece, her high-pitched coital cries, the prolonged and tender and unhoped-for meditations of her mouth upon his phallus.*

What Mindy and I didn't know then was that John Updike and Philip Roth were pioneers who were irrevocably changing the rules. Their two books, one quintessentially WASPy, the other quintessentially Jewish, both totally modern American in their unrelenting preoccupation with and exploration of sexuality, were pushing erotica to the center stage of serious American fiction.

Today, not only have explicit sexual descriptions become an integral part of American literature, but our best authors have elevated erotica to art. Forget pulp fiction. What Mr. Feingold once referred to as the good parts can be found in writers the caliber of Toni Morrison, E. L. Doctorow, Mary Gordon, Don DeLillo, and Joyce Carol Oates—to name just five. Thanks to the serious dedication of authors like these to their art and to the truth, you don't have to take the train to Flushing to find out about sex.

It wasn't always like this—writers who devoted a portion of their talent to writing about sex were viewed as giving in to their prurient side, or they wrote in such a veiled style that the effect tread precariously on the line between the artful and the ludicrous. Consider this passage (speaking of trains) from Frederick Wakeman's post-war novel, *The Hucksters:*

It was true what he said about trains. A man wants a woman. Is restless for a woman. It is a much stronger feeling than any other travel feeling. So men drink, play cards, talk their heads off—but none of it helps the loneliness for women. That is why it is hard to read, impossible to work, on a train. A man says the shifting light is hard on his eyes or that he hates being cooped up, but the fact is he wants to concentrate on a woman and nothing else. He is only happy on a train with a woman. The best relief from his longing is gambling, but even gambling for higher stakes than he can afford is a poor excuse for not finding a woman.

It is an entirely competent piece of writing and true about what it says and as far as it goes. The problem is that it doesn't go far enough, and that keeps it from being a memorable passage. Think of what a John Updike or a Philip Roth could do with a situation like this. Updike would give us a specific woman, the smell of her perfume, the texture of her sweater, and perhaps the cool grandeur in the angle of her face as she responds to club-car conversation. Roth might give us a fantasy (perhaps masturbatory) and recount it with such a fiercely obsessive *knowing* intelligence that the scene would be immediately compelling. Is it unfair to compare Wakeman to Updike or Roth? It would be, but what is being compared is not the abilities of these writers, but the license they believed they had to express themselves and depict sexual themes. And, of course, that license is granted by readers who accept or reject those expressions, so we are, in the final analysis, comparing what readers found acceptable in the art of fiction and what they found pornographic. Wakeman's ad men are properly remembered as titillating and provocative by the readers of that pre–Augie March day, who derived more from the reticence of the writing than from its explicitness.

THIS ANTHOLOGY COLLECTS ABOUT FIFTY OF THE BEST EX-amples of American erotic writing from the last fifty years or so. Although I've included a few excerpts that broke new ground in the past, the emphasis is strongly on the contemporary. The fact is that, while certain aspects of sexual behavior may never change, and "a kiss is still a kiss," there are elements of how we behave toward one another during moments of intimacy that are products of the time. Perhaps it's the influence of movies and television, or Madison Avenue and the tabloids, but there are all sorts of admixtures of urges and images taking place in our psyches that affect how we act. Writers are not particularly adept at understanding the dynamics of all this, but that's not their job. They're simply telling us how we are and how the outpouring of these mixtures spills across the terrain of our lives. As this anthology shows, I think, practitioners of fiction are the best at this.

Chronologically, I decided to start the collection with Saul

Bellow. There are three reasons for this. First, he is indisputably one of America's great writers. Second, *The Adventures of Augie March* is a fiercely American work. It's an exuberant, sprawling, panoramic picaresque that boisterously—and totally unapologetically—embraces a riotous, tumultuous, and often energetically criminal America. Third, more than any writer of his generation, Bellow's work is characterized by his insistent belief that the territory of the serious fiction writer includes any and all aspects of real life. "I go after reality with words," he once said (raffishly, it seems to me). Reality of course includes sexuality. Yet when *The Adventures of Augie March* exploded onto the scene in 1953, so-called serious writing in the United States was still dominated by staid, middlebrow artificiality. Nowhere was this more evident than in the almost total lack of intelligent erotica. Finally, it's worth noting that the year the book was published Philip Roth was twenty, John Updike was twenty-one, and E. L. Doctorow was twenty-two. Change was coming.

More than half of the entries in this collection are by women. I did not set out to do that; it just turned out that way. It's no overstatement to say that with an astounding variety of viewpoints and a rich diversity of styles, contemporary women writers have not just revitalized but totally reinvented erotic fiction. The best of their work is not only highly provocative, it is also utterly new. Condescending generalities of the past like "woman's perspective" and "female point of view" have become (finally) totally obsolete. Today it would be ridiculous to try and single out a fiction writer who expresses "the woman's perspective." Is it Mary Gordon, Mary Gaitskill, or

Mary Caponegro? There are as many female points of view as there are women writing about sexuality.

Here are two passages about couples. One is by Robb Foreman Dew, the other is by Joyce Carol Oates. Let me tell you which is which on the other side of them and see if they don't make my point for me.

But later, when they finally settled themselves in the same bed, they were both made easier by their instinctive inclination to turn toward the other. Each one had expected that the other would be too tired to make love. In fact, they made love with a gentle and slow pleasure, because their energy was not great. Their passion was not ragged or insistent, and Dinah was glad that her body was allowing her this great enjoyment; she wasn't hindered by vanity or self-evaluation; she was not being judged. The two of them were such good and comfortable partners; their instincts were always reliable, so that they lay in bed after making love satisfied and no longer needful in any way, for the time being. Dinah was thinking that sex can be the sweetest, kindest way finally to overcome reticence. They both felt at ease at last, and in the morning they were fond and affectionate with each other and with the children.

And the second:

He took her to a hotel on Seventh Avenue. Not one of the better hotels—because he hadn't much cash with him that day, and didn't care to use his credit card; and because, in a better hotel, the girl's noisy exuberance might have attracted attention.

Her arms were like steel bands around his neck and back. She screamed, she wept, she rolled her head from side to side, in a transport of passion—so clearly unfeigned!—that excited him more violently than he had been excited in many years.

And then, afterward, she had not wanted him to move from her.

"No, no," she said hoarsely, angrily, "no, I want you there, I want you there, I'll kill you if you leave—"

So he lay on top of her, vastly flattered, sweating, his heart hammering in his chest, his thoughts racing so crazily they were colored paper streamers, razor-thin strips of confetti.

"Don't you leave me don't you ever leave me or I'll kill you—I swear I'll kill you—" The girl shouted.

As you might have expected (but not if I hadn't warned you), the first is by Dew and the second is by Oates.

ONE THING I DISCOVERED IN PUTTING TOGETHER THESE selections is that erotica is responsible for some of the most interesting long sentences in the English language. I could be wrong, but it sometimes seems to me that these authors are in the throes of some kind of aroused state (to put it nicely) that expresses itself in the gushing forth of words, commas, and semi-colons, all building up to the climactic and finally restful period. Here are Philip Roth, Harold Brodkey, and Robert Olen Butler, respectively; see if you think I'm onto something.

To be sure, I must first accustom myself to what strikes me at the height of my skepticism as so much theatrical display; but soon, as understanding grows, as familiarity grows, and feeling with it, I begin at last to relinquish some of my suspiciousness, to lay off a little with my interrogations, and to see these passionate performances as arising out of the very fearlessness that so draws me to her, out of that determined abandon with which she will give herself to whatever strongly beckons, and regardless of how likely it is to bring in the end as much pain as pleasure.

Any attempted act confers vulnerability on you, but an act devoted to her pleasure represented doubled vulnerability since only she could judge it; and I was safe only if I was immune or insensitive to her; but if I was immune or insensitive I could not hope to help her come; by making myself vulnerable to her, I was in a way being a sissy or a creep because Orra wasn't organized or trained or prepared to accept responsibility for how I felt about myself; she was a woman who wanted to be left alone; she was paranoid about the inroads on her life men in their egos tried to make: there was dangerous masochism, dangerous hubris, dangerous hopefulness, and a form of love in my doing what I did: I nuzzled nakedly at the crotch of the sexual tigress; any weakness in her ego or her judgment and she would lash out at me, and the line was very frail between what I was doing as love and as intrusion, exploitation, and stupid boastfulness.

And down at the end of the long drive there was a pothole and a road crew and a cauldron mixing tar with the smell of tar a girl rides past me on her bike and she has long russet hair and she is barefoot and I am ten years old and I stand beneath the horse chestnut tree in my yard and watch her go by and it is early summer, school is out and all the summer lies ahead and somewhere in the direction she's heading, a street is being resurfaced and the smell of tar is in the air and I run to my bike and I race after her, watching the lift of her hair behind her and she is willow thin and her bare heels rise and fall and rise and fall and the smell of tar grows stronger and she turns at the corner and I turn and ahead the street is slick black and at the far end the dump truck has just whooshed into emptiness and stops in a cloud of gravel dust and I've been thinking all along about how to overtake her, how to speak to her, and miraculously she stops ahead and gets off and nudges her kick-stand down with the ball of her pretty foot and already I have the instinct from this moment of enchantment looking at her summer-bare feet to follow the line from her instep up her ankle up her leg to the sweet subtlety of her knee to her thigh and then to vague thoughts of things that are still as secret to me as the origin of the universe.

After those, this fifty-four-word sentence from Jennifer Egan—"Yet even now, even amidst that hopelessness, Phoebe still wanted more; she was two people, one despairing, the other greedy and low, overjoyed when Wolf roused himself and moved down to stroke her with his mouth — the sensations were murderous, unbearable, she came almost instantly, like being smacked in the head and losing consciousness." — seems almost terse by comparison.

NO BRIEF INTRODUCTIONS COULD BEGIN TO DO JUSTICE TO the rich diversity and often startling originality of erotica in contemporary American fiction. For those who would like to chart the development of American fiction's handling of sexual themes, the book ends with a chronological listing of authors and titles. This listing will make it clear that some of the best material of this kind is of pretty recent vintage. Today's best work includes both the sacred and the profane. It ranges from the warmly sensual to the achingly tender, from the playfully perverse to the deeply poignant. There is dazzling exultant lyricism as well as icily ironic lucidity. There is both delicacy and daring, rapacity and repose. I, for one, can't wait to see where the writers of tomorrow will take this.

I hope you enjoy the collection. Some of the selections may seem very brief — I guess for those I imagined Mindy looking up and reading me a passage from the novel she was into at the moment — and others are longer. There should be something here for everyone or almost everyone. Considering that this is a book that purports to be filled with good parts, neither I nor Mr. Feingold would find it amiss if several selections or passages were marked for future reference.

Preface

I am extremely grateful to those people who brought writers and works to my attention: Agnes Darrin, Martha Sternwood, and John Klotzbach. I would also like to thank Judith Torgerson, Gianni Polizzi, Mimi R., Alberto W., Carol Spillone Mueller, Samantha Greene, Regan Park, and most of all, Alex Hoyt and Harold Rabinowitz for their infinite patience and unfailingly good-humored encouragement.

Princeton, New Jersey—April 1998

Chronology

1988 — Michael Chabon *The Mysteries of Pittsburgh*

1989 — Robert Boswell *The Geography of Desire*

1989 — E. L. Doctorow *Billy Bathgate*

1989 — Mary Gordon *The Other Side*

1989 — Oscar Hijuelos *The Mambo Kings Play Songs of Love*

1989 — Susanna Moore *The Whiteness of Bones*

1989 — Pam Durban "World of Women"

1990 — Dani Shapiro *Playing with Fire*

1990 — Frederick Busch *Harry and Catherine*

1990 — Mary Caponegro "The Star Cafe"

1990 — A. M. Homes "Chunky in Heat" from *The Safety of Objects*

1990 — Charles Johnson *Middle Passage*

1991 — Jane Smiley *A Thousand Acres*

1992 — Robert Olen Butler *They Whisper*

1992 — Siri Hustvedt *The Blindfold*

1992 — Susan Sontag *The Volcano Lover*

1993 — Amy Bloom "Only You"

1993 — Steve Erickson *ARC d'X*

1993 — Amanda Filipacchi *Nude Men*

1993 — Anna Monardo *The Courtyard of Dreams*

1993 — Maria Flook *Family Night*

1993 — Dale Peck *Martin and John*

1993 — Joan Wickersham *The Paper Anniversary*

1994 — Lynne McFall *Dancer with Bruised Knees*

1994 — Gwendolyn M. Parker *These Same Long Bones*

1995 — Charles D'Ambrosio "Lyricism"

1995 — Jennifer Egan *The Invisible Circus*

1995 — Anchee Min *Katherine*

1995 — Rick Moody "The Ring of Brightest Angels Around Heaven"

1995 — Charlotte Watson Sherman *Touch*

1995 — Paula Huston *Daughters of Song*

1996 — James McManus *Going to the Sun*

1997 — Mary Gaitskill "Processing" from *Because They Wanted To*

"Kathy Goes to Haiti"

Novelist Kathy Acker is an audacious original. She consistently subverts traditional narrative with unrelenting anarchic energy and passionate post-punk feminism. Her writing is daring, sexy, and smart. This excerpt is from her novel Literal Madness.

HE GETS UP TO GO TO THE BATHROOM. KATHY HEARS HIM piss. "Come here."

She walks into the bathroom and sees him sitting on the toilet. "Sit on me."

She sits down slowly, her back facing him. His cock slides up her asshole. His hands grab her tits.

She wonders if he's still going to the bathroom. "Shit and piss," she thinks to herself, "Fuck and suck what and not."

Everything's everything else. Kathy's crouching behind the window, watching the gray cat stalk someone she can't see. "Let's go to bed," Roger says.

He takes Kathy's hand and leads her to the bed.

Lays her back down on the bed. "This bed makes too much noise."

"It's just a lousy bed."

"Let's move it away from the wall."

"Do I have to get up?"

"No." He pulls the bed away from the wall so the wood headboard doesn't bang against the wall and lies down. His head is on Kathy's cunt. He sticks his tongue in Kathy's cunt and licks. Then he raises his head. His dark brown beard hairs are rubbing the lighter brown wet cunt hairs. Roger's beard hairs are partly white from sucking Kathy.

She moans.

"Now do you like my beard?" Roger asks.

"I always liked your beard."

"But now you see why my beard's so special."

"Oh shit." Kathy's heat's rising. She's about to come again. Roger doesn't want her to come again from his tongue. He rises over Kathy and sticks his cock into her cunt.

Kathy doesn't exactly know what's happening. Roger and Kathy fuck and then stop fuck and then stop fuck and then stop. They're actually fucking slowly and in a steady rhythm. Kathy's cunt is so sore that Kathy comes whenever Roger's cock is inside her. Yet they're fucking slowly enough that she's not becoming hysterical. Fucking is not fucking and not fucking is fucking. No one can tell who's coming or who's not coming. No one knows and forgets anything.

"Will you really come to Le Roi tomorrow?"

"I said I would," laughing.

"What haven't you done in bed?"

"I don't know. If I knew, I'd do it. Oh, I've never really gotten tied up and beaten or tied up and beaten someone, though I've thought about it a lot. Have you?"

"Oh yes. I once went with a girl the only way she could get off was if I tied her up and hit her. Otherwise she didn't want it, no way. I tied her wrists behind her back. I hit her hard. When she was ready she'd be writhing and shaking and then she'd want it so bad."

"You didn't like it?"

"It was OK. I didn't care for it that much. Did you ever ass fuck?"

"Jesus Christ, we were ass fucking when we were on the toilet. Couldn't you tell?"

"I was so hot, all I could think about was getting my own. I don't even know if you've been coming."

"I've been coming enough. I'm satisfied."

"I want to fuck you up the ass when I know it."

"I like to fuck women. I don't do it much anymore though I used to."

"I like when women make love with women."

"Have you ever made it with a man?"

"I wouldn't let a man near me. I know what I want," Roger says.

"What do you want?"

"Are you really going to come to Le Roi?"

"I said I was going to. Jesus Christ, I'm here 'cause I want to see as much of Haiti as possible."

"I'd love to have you make love to my wife. That's why I want you to come to Le Roi."

"Waaiit a minute. I don't go for women all that much and I definitely only go for women I want. I don't even know Betty. I'd like to meet Betty 'cause she's an American and 'cause she sounds pretty damn lonely, but that's it."

"Maybe you and her will get something together. I want to find a woman who'll make love to my wife. That's what Betty needs."

"Roger, even if Betty and I do do anything, that's between me and Betty. It's none of your business. What goes on between you and Betty doesn't concern me. Jesus Christ, I don't even know Betty yet."

"I don't believe you're going to come to Le Roi tomorrow."

"How do I get to Le Roi?"

"Everyone in town knows where Le Roi is. You can ask anyone. There's a bridge and there's a big red chimney. The big red chimney's Le Roi."

"On the way to the airport?"

"Yes."

"I guess I'll find it."

"What time will you come?"

"About one o'clock."

"I'll wait for you. My father's rebuilding the factory. He has three new rum tanks. I'll show you the rum tanks, and then I'll take you in to meet Betty."

"Are you sure it'll be OK with Betty? I don't know if she wants to meet me."

"The only way Betty ever meets people is when I introduce them to her."

Roger and Kathy look at each other. Their lips meet. Roger

sticks his cock into Kathy's overfucked cunt. Roger comes. Kathy feels every inch of his cock spasm back and forth as clearly as she sees the white ceiling above her. Roger's orgasm makes Kathy hot.

They stop fucking. Roger's cock is hard again. Roger wets his finger and sticks it into Kathy's ass. His finger moves around easily. He sloshes some saliva on the asshole and eases his cock into Kathy's ass. Kathy doesn't feel any pain at all.

Roger's moving his cock back and forth rapidly. Kathy's coming like a maniac. All of her ass and intestinal muscles are shaking. "Oh oh oh," Kathy cries. Kathy stops coming. Roger's still shaking away. Kathy feels a little pain. Kathy and Roger both come again.

The Adventures of
Augie March

Many people remember where they were and what they were doing when they read The Adventures of Augie March—*the way people remember where they were when they heard about Pearl Harbor or when the lights went out during the great blackout. The style of the book is as free and breezy as the way the hero careens through America of the post-war period. Bellow was among the first to see how life—externally, but internally as well, in the guise of attitudes and values—had changed radically after the war. The writing of fiction took a sharp turn after* Augie March, *and no one could have written in the same way after 1953—about life, sex, money, love, work, . . . or anything—even if Bellow had not gone on to win the Nobel Prize in literature in 1976.*

BUT THERE WERE PEOPLE AT THE TABLE NEAR THEIRS THAT soon were of more interest to me—two young girls, of beauty to put a stop to such thoughts or drive them to the dwindling point. There was a moment when I could have fallen for either one of them, and then everything bent to one side, toward the slenderer, slighter, younger one. I fell in love with her, and not in the way I had loved Hilda Novinson either, going like a satellite on the back of the streetcar or sticking around her father's tailor shop. This time I had a different kind of maniac energy and knew what sexual sting was. My expectations were greater; more corrupt too, maybe, owing to the influence of Mrs. Renling and her speaking always of lusts, no holds barred. So that I allowed suggestions in all veins to come to me. I never have learned to reproach myself for such things; and then my experience in curtailing them was limited. Why, I had accepted of Grandma Lausch's warning only the part about the danger of our blood and that, through Mama, we were susceptible to love; not the stigmatizing part that made us out the carriers of the germ of ruination. So I was dragged, entrained, over a barrel. And I had a special handicap, because of the way I presented myself—due to Mrs. Renling—as if God had not left out a single one of His gifts, and I was advertising His liberality with me: good looks, excellent wardrobe, mighty fine manners, social ease, wittiness, handsome-devil smiles, neat dancing and address with women—all in the freshest gold-leaf. And the trouble was that I had what you might call forged credentials. It was my worry that Esther Fenchet would find this out.

I worked, heart-choked, for the grandest success in these limits, as an impostor. I spent hours getting myself up to be a living petition. By dumb concentration and notice-wooing struggle. The only way I could conceive, in my blood-loaded, picturesque amorousness. But, the way a hint of plague is

given in the mild wind of flags and beauty of a harbor—a
scene of safe, busy peace—I could perhaps, for all of my sane
look of easy, normal circumstances, have passed the note of
my thoughts in the air—on the beach, on the flower-cultured
lawn, in the big open of the white and gold dining room—
and these thoughts were that I could submit to being hung in
the girl's hair—of that order. I had heavy dreams about her
lips, hands, breasts, legs, between legs. She could not stoop for
a ball on the tennis court—I standing stiff in a foulard with
brown horses on a green background that was ingeniously
slipped through a handcarved wooden ring which Renling
made popular that season in Evanston—I couldn't witness this,
I say, without a push of love and worship in my bowels at the
curve of her lips, and triumphant maiden shape behind, and
soft, protected secret. Where, to be allowed with love, would
be the endorsement of the world, that it was not the barren
confusion distant dry fears hinted and whispered, but was necessary, justified, the justification proved by joy. That if she
would have, to prove, kiss, use her hands on me, allow me the
clay dust of the court from her legs, the mild sweat, her intimate dirt and sweat, deliver me from suffering falsehood—
show that there wasn't anything false, injurious, or empty-
hearted that couldn't be corrected!

But in the evening, when nothing had come of my effort,
a scoreless day, I lay on the floor of my room, all dressed up
to go to dinner, with doomed patience, eaten with hankering
and thinking futilely what brilliant thing to do—some floral,
comet, star action, casting off stupidity and clumsiness. But I
had marked carefully all that I could about Esther, in order to

study what could induce her to see herself with me, in my light. That is, up there in sublimity. Asking only that she join me, let me, ride and row in love with me, with her fresh, great female wonders and beauties which would increase by my joy that she was exactly as she was, with her elbows, her nipples at her sweater. I watched how she chased a little awkwardly on the tennis court and made to protect her breasts and closed in her knees when a fast ball came over the net. My study of her didn't much support my hopes; which was why I lay on the floor with a desiring, sunburned face and lips open in thought. I realized that she knew she had great value, and that she was not subject to urgent-heartedness. In short, that Esther Fenchel was not of my persuasion and wouldn't much care to hear about her perspiration and little personal dirts. . . .

. . . AND THEN HE FETCHED UP HIS GIRL—A BIG DARK GIRL named Cissy Flexner. I had known her at school; she was from the neighborhood. Her father, before he went bust, had owned a drygoods store—overalls, laborers' canvas gloves and long-johns, galoshes, things like that; and he was a fleshy, diffident, pale, inside sort of man, back in his boxes. But she, although in a self-solicitous way, was a beautiful piece of tall work, on colossal but careful legs, hips forward; her mouth was big and would have been perfect if there hadn't been something self-tasting in it, eyes with complicated lids but magnificent in their slow heaviness, an erotic development. So that she had to cast down these eyes a little to be decent with her endowment, that height of the bosom and form of hips and other genetic riches, smooth and soft, that may take the early person, the little girl, by surprise in their ampleness when they come on. She accused me somewhat of examining her too much, but could anybody help that? And it was excusable on the further score that she might become my sister-in-law, for Simon was powerfully in love. He already was husbandly toward her, and they hung on each other with fondling and kissing and intimacy, strolling by the steep colors of water and air, while I swam by myself in the lake a little distance away. Also on the sand, when Simon, after he had rubbed his fine shield of chest hair, dried her back, he kissed it, and it gave me a moment's ache in the roof of the mouth, as if I had got the warm odor and touch of skin myself. She had so much, gave out so much splendor. As stupendous quiff.

But personally I didn't care too much for her. Partly because I was gone on Esther. But also because what came across as her own, that is, apart from female brilliance, was slow. Maybe she herself was stupefied by what she had, her slaying weight. It must have pressed down on her thoughts like any great vitality in nature. Like the aims that live in the blood of grizzly or tiger, bearing down on the mind of such beasts with square weight, a manifestation of one thing carried out completely, to the very stripes and claws. But what about the privilege over that of being in the clasp of nature, and in on the mission of a species? The ingredient of thought was weaker in Cissy's mixture than the other elements. But she was a sly girl, soft though she seemed.

And as she lay stretched on the sand, and the hot oil of popcorn and sharpness of mustard came in puffs, with crackling, from the stands of Silver Beach, she kept answering Simon, whom I couldn't hear—he was on his side next to her in his red trunks—"Oh, fooey, no. What bushwah! Love, shmuv!" But her pleasure was high. "I'm so glad you brought me, dear. So clean. It's heavenly here."

I didn't like Simon's struggle with her—for that was what it was—to convince her, sway her, work her around. Nearly everything he proposed she refused. "Let's not and say we did," and similar denials. It led him into crudenesses I hadn't ever seen him in before, the way he laid himself out, dug, campaigned, swashed, flattered her, was gross. His tongue hung out with the heat of work and infatuation; and there was a bottom ground where he was angry, his anger rising straight into his face in two flaming centers, under his eyes, on either side of his nose. I understood this, as we were covering the same field of difficulty and struggle in front of the identical Troy. This that happened to us would have given Grandma Lausch the satisfaction of a prophetess—the spirit, anyhow, of her; the actual was covered up in the dust of the Home, in the band of finalists for whom there was the little guessing game of which would next be taken out of play. So I recorded this seeming success of prediction for her. And as for Simon, all the places where he and I had once been joined while still young brothers, before there were differences and distances between us—these places began to act up, feeling, attachment near again. The reattachment didn't actually take place, but I loved him nevertheless.

When he was on his feet with the flowered cloth of her beach dress on his shoulders, it made something crass but brave, his standing up raw and sunburned, by the pure streak of the water, as if he were being playful about the wearing of this girl's favor.

I took them to the evening steamer, for she refused to stay overnight, and was on deck with them through the long working out of sunset, down to the last blue, devoid of other lights; fall weight and furrows in the clouds set cityward, let go from the power of the sun to sink down on the moundings and pilings of the water, gray and powerful.

"Well, sport, we may be married in the next few months," he said. "You envy me? I bet you do."

And he covered her up with his hands and arms, his chin on her shoulder and kissing her on the neck. The flamboyant way he had of making love to her was curious to me—his leg advanced between her legs and his fingers spread on her face. She didn't refuse anything he did, although in words never agreed; she had no kindness in speaking. With her hands up the sleeves of her white coat, hugging out the chill, she stood by a davit. He was still in his shirt, owing to sunburn, but wore his panama, the breeze molding the brim around.

"Only You"

Amy Bloom is a psychotherapist who divides her time between her practice and her writing. She is the author of a collection of short stories, Come to Me, *which was a National Book Award finalist, and a novel,* Love Invents Us. *Always intelligent, always compassionate, her work has the power to both disturb and soothe. This passage is from the short story "Only You." Amy Bloom lives in Durham, Connecticut.*

"TO MY DARLING MARIE, THE MOST BEAUTIFUL WOMAN IN North Carolina."

Marie blushes with pleasure and looks down at the hem of her ivory dressing gown.

"What would you like?" Alvin asks, his voice so soft that Marie isn't sure what he's saying.

"I have everything I want. This has been the most wonderful three days of my life, and I owe it all to you."

Alvin smiles and kisses her hand.

"What would you like?" she asks, knowing that whatever he says, she wants to give it to him. Even if what he wants is sex, she wants to give it to him, never mind Henry, never mind her own well-known lack of interest, which is at this very moment dissolving.

Alvin tells her that what he wants is to dress in her clothes, in her lingerie, that she is so beautiful he wants to feel what it is to be her, to be even closer to her. He looks right into her eyes at first, but he ends by looking down into the courtyard. Marie has no idea what to say, she refuses even to think the hurtful words that Henry would use. Whatever Alvin wants, she wants to give him. She nods her head, hoping that that is enough.

Alvin walks over to the dresser and takes out a chemise and a half-slip and a pair of pantyhose. Marie watches the waves beyond the terrace. She doesn't trust her own face.

Alvin goes into the bathroom, wanting not to frighten Marie, wanting not to embarrass either one of them. He knows what he needs to do. Slowly, he sweeps foundation up from his jawline, over his high cheekbones, all the way back to his ears, making sure there's no line on his neck. He takes out a new, sharp-edged pink lipstick, brushes on one coat, presses a Kleenex to his lips, and puts on a second coat to last. He doesn't do much with his small blue eyes, just a little dark brown mascara and the pale rose eye shadow he's taught Marie to use, to make her eyes look brighter. He passes the blush-on brush over his cheeks lightly.

Alvin pauses, looking at himself, closing his eyes a little. There's so much he can't fix, can't fix right now, anyway. He takes out the wig he bought in Germany five years ago, six hundred dollars' worth of beautiful long blond hair, no frizzy

polyester, just some young fraulein's decision to go short one
summer, and there it was. He puts on the pantyhose and the
half-slip and the matching chemise he had persuaded Marie
to buy, hoping that he would be wearing it with her. He wraps
his navy silk robe around him and finds the navy silk mules
he got while picking out the ivory ones for Marie. He loves
Marie's small round feet and spares himself the sight of his
own well-shaped but too large feet sliding into the heels. If he
wore anything larger than a ten, he would go barefoot rather
than be one of those jumbo transvestites, big-knuckled hands
made pathetic by pale pink nail polish, thick necks hidden by
carefully tossed scarves. Alvin lets himself think only about
Marie, about how much she loves him and admires him. He
knows she does. You can fake a lot of things, Alvin knows, but
you can't fake love. He adjusts the wig quickly, tucking up his
light brown bangs, and walks out of the bathroom, away from
the mirror, toward Marie.

Marie has turned down the lights and drawn the sheer white
curtains closed. In the gold, shining moonlight, Alvin really
looks, for one moment, like a pretty woman, strong-
shouldered, with a narrow waist and long legs under her rustling silk robe.

"You look beautiful," Marie says.

"Marie, angel, right now, I feel beautiful. I feel like you.
You know I think you're a beautiful, beautiful woman. I want
us to be closer. I want to be very close, okay?"

They look at each other directly, breathing uncertainty and
tenderness. Alvin kneels down, carefully, hoping he won't tip
over in his heels, and he removes Marie's ivory slippers. He

takes her by the hand and lays her down on the bedspread. To make love, Marie relaxes a little more; when Henry wants to make love he always pulls the covers back.

Marie cannot stand to watch Alvin's lipsticked mouth moving down her breast, but she responds to its warm shape, pressing and gently tugging. The muscles in her back ripple, and her brown hair flutters like the leaves of a small bronze tree in the wind. As the tips of his long blond hair brush lightly across her chest Alvin looks up just in time to see Marie's slight, astonished smile, and he pulls her closer, opening her robe.

"Beautiful," he whispers.

"Beautiful," she says.

-⟨ ROBERT BOSWELL ⟩-

The Geography
of Desire

Robert Boswell was born in Missouri and educated at the University of Arizona in Tucson. He has taught creative writing at both the University of Arizona and Northwestern, and is currently an assistant professor of English at New Mexico State University. He has written a collection of short stories, Dancing in the Movies, *and four novels,* Crooked Hearts, Mystery Ride, The Geography of Desire, *and* America Owned Love. *He is married to the writer Antonya Nelson. This excerpt is from* The Geography of Desire, *a potent mix of sensuality, strangeness, and intrigue.*

HE COULD NOT HAVE GUESSED THE EXTENT OF LOURDES'S fascination concerning Pilar. Daily, while she worked dough across a table, counted change, cleaned the black oven, even now while she stood on the balcony without him, Lourdes pictured Pilar as precisely as she was able, troubling herself over the smallest details—the part of her hair, the lift of her lips, the curve of her brows, the sway in her shoulders as she walked. She knew Pilar possessed a quality that made her different from others, a quality Lourdes could not name. Certainly she was pretty, but that wasn't all of it. Hadn't everyone said that she, Lourdes, was pretty too? Even Pilar admitted it. There was some additional quality, an elusive one.

From her bedroom in the rear of the bakery, Lourdes had watched Leon walk with Pilar along the edge of the water. They had held hands, conversing with Ramon, although Lourdes had been unable to hear more than an occasional word. The walk had seemed aimless, but there had been one moment Lourdes could not forget. The three of them had lain in the sand separately, each gesturing to the other, wallowing around. Then Pilar had stretched her arms from one man to the other, and at that instant, everything changed: Their moods seemed to alter, their movements became graceful, the men suddenly relaxed and turned toward Pilar, everything—even the color of the sky, the taste of the breeze off the ocean, the quality of the moonlight on the radiant shore—everything had become new. Lourdes had watched it happen, and then suddenly, as if by magic, Pilar's skirt inflated before them, and she lifted her perfect brown legs toward the sky. Lourdes had felt her heart stop.

Since witnessing that moment, she'd known that Pilar possessed knowledge she did not have, and she wanted it. Lourdes was not going to give Leon up.

The apron flew into the room from the balcony, its strings trailing like streamers. Sandals, one at a time, sailed through the slant of sunlight and bounced off the far wall.

"I believe I'll undress out here," she called.

Leon took a cigarette from the pack on the dresser. "Do you want a smoke?"

She entered unbuttoning the slate blouse with one hand, holding the novel with the other. "I like this book." She pulled on the tail of her shirt, freeing it of the yellow skirt. An old bra, straps attached by safety pins, crossed her chest like a solemn promise.

"I don't think it's all that good," he said, the cigarette in his mouth but unlit. "I should have bought you something I already knew."

Her blouse fell. She pulled the bra over her head. Her breasts, though small, were perfectly round.

Leon flicked the cigarette across the bed to the floor, sat up on his knees, and kissed those breasts while her hands moved through his hair. The latch on her skirt was tricky, but he remembered it and undid it expertly. The skirt slid down her legs. Her underwear, dirty with a hole at either hip, made him wonder at the layers of her clothing—the filthy apron, the clean blouse and skirt, her frayed bra and tattered panties. He tugged the panties down.

Making love with Lourdes was an athletic contest, and Leon sometimes imagined it as literally that—an Olympic event complete with judges who would hold up cards to indicate his score. He never felt more that he represented his country than when in bed with her. It was a battle of wills and strength, both invigorating and tiresome. In this particular match, she wrestled him beneath her, digging her nails into his wrists. He locked his right leg around her left, then rolled her onto her side. He was stronger than she, but barely. He kissed her neck, she bit his ear, and he entered her as she pitched toward him. The judges would have been pleased.

Lourdes believed sex should be furious, dramatic. Leon believed the man should please the woman. He flung himself against her, biting her nipples. She struggled against him one moment, then lifted her bottom to meet him the next. When they finished, they were both exhausted, pleased from sexual fulfillment and relieved at successful conclusion. This encounter ended with Lourdes laughing.

"Innocence"

Harold Brodkey will (it seems) be forever as well known for his quarter-century-long case of writer's block as for his articulate and sensitive fiction, nearly all in the form of short stories. After a widely acclaimed debut collection of stories, First Love and Other Sorrows, *Brodkey fell into the grips of a confused ennui from which he could not extricate himself until the publication of* Women and Angels *in 1985. The 1988 publication of* Stories in an Almost Classical Mode, *in which this story appeared, reestablished his reputation as a master of the short form. Although he never made any excuses or claimed to be making a point, Brodkey's block might be seen as a failure—or metaphor for one—of readers to feel, to sense, and to read. He died in 1996 of AIDS, carefully documenting his struggle against the disease in the pages of* The New Yorker.

I STARTED MANIPULATING HER DELICATELY WITH MY HAND; and in my own excitement, and thinking she was ready, I sort of scrambled up and, covering her with myself, and playing with her with one hand, guided my other self, my lower consciousness, into her. My God, she was warm and restless inside; it was heated in there and smooth, insanely smooth, and oiled, and full of movements. But I knew at once I'd made a mistake: I should have gone on licking her; there were no regular contractions; she was anxious for the prick, she rose around it, closed around it, but in a rigid, dumb, far-away way; and her twitchings played on it, ran through it, through the walls of it and into me; and they were uncontrolled and not exciting, but empty; she didn't know what to do, how to be fucked and come. I couldn't pull out of her, I didn't want to, I couldn't pull out; but if there were no contractions for me to respond to, how in hell would I find the rhythm for her? I started slowly with what seemed infinite suggestiveness to me, with great dirtiness, a really grown-up sort of fucking—just in case she was far along—and she let out a huge, shuddering hour-long sigh and cried out my name and then in a sobbing, exhausted voice, said, "I lost it . . . Oh Wiley, I lost it . . . Let's stop . . ." My face was above hers; her face was wet with tears; why was she crying like that? She had changed her mind; now she wanted to come; she turned her head back and forth; she said, "I'm no good . . . I'm no good . . . Don't worry about me . . . You come . . ."

No matter what I mumbled, "Hush," and "Don't be silly," and in a whisper, "Orra, I love you," she kept on saying those things until I slapped her lightly and said, *"Shut up, Orra."*

Then she was silent again.

The thing was, apparently, that she was arrhythmic: at least that's what I thought; and that meant there weren't going to be regular contractions, any rhythm for me to follow; and any rhythm I set up as I fucked, she broke with her movements: so that it was that when she moved, she made her excitement go away: it would be best if she moved very smally: but I was afraid to tell her that, or even to try to hold her hips firmly, and guide them, to instruct her in that way for fear she'd get self-conscious and lose what momentum she'd won. And also I was ashamed that I'd stopped going down on her. I experimented — doggedly, sweatily, to make up for what I'd done — with fucking in different ways, and I fantasized about us being in Mexico, some place warm and lushly colored where we made love easily and filthily and graphically. The fantasy kept me going. That is, it kept me hard. I kept acting out an atmosphere of sexual pleasure — I mean of my sexual pleasure — for her to rest on, so she could count on that. I discovered that a not very slow sort of one-one-one stroke, or fuck-fuck-fuck-Orra-now-now-now really got to her; her feelings would grow heated; and she could shift up from that with me into a one-two, one-two, one-two, her excitement rising; but if she or I then tried to shift up farther to one-two-three, one-two-three, one-two-three, she'd lose it all. That was too complicated for her: my own true love, my white American. But her feelings when they were present were very strong, they came in gusts, huge squalls of heat as if from a furnace with a carelessly banging door, and they excited and allured both of us. That excitement and the dit-dit-ditting got to her; she began to be generally, continuingly sexual. It's almost standard to compare sexual excitement to holiness; well, after a while, holiness seized her; she spoke with tongues, she testified. She was shaking all over; she was saved temporarily and sporadically; that is, she kept lapsing out of that excitement too. But it would recur. Her hands would flutter; her face would be pale and then red, then very, very red; her eyes would stare at nothing; she'd call my name. I'd plug on one-one-one, then one-two, one-two, then I'd go back to one-one-one: I could see as before—in the deep pleasure I felt even in the midst of the labor—why a man might kill her in order to stimulate in her (although he might not know this was why he did it) these signs of pleasure. The familiar Orra had vanished; she said, "GodohGodohGod"; it was sin and redemption and holiness and visions time. Her throbs were very direct, easily comprehensible, but without any pattern; they weren't in any regular sequence; still, they were exciting to me, maybe all the more exciting because of the piteousness of her not being able to regulate them, of their being like blows delivered inside her by an enemy whom she couldn't even half-domesticate or make friendly to herself or speak to. She was the most out-of-control girl I ever screwed. She would at times start to thrust like a woman who had her sexuality readied and well-understood at last and I'd start to distend with anticipation and a pride and relief as large as a house; but after two thrusts— or four, or six—she'd have gotten too excited, she'd be shaking, she'd thrust crookedly and out of tempo, the movement would collapse; or she'd suddenly jerk in mid-movement without warning and crash around with so great and so meaningless a violence that she'd lose her thing; and she'd start to cry. She'd whisper wetly, "I lost it"; so I'd say, "No you didn't," and I'd go on or start over, one-one-one; and of course, the excitement would come back; sometimes it came back at once; but she was increasingly afraid of herself, afraid to move her lower body; she would try to hold still and just *receive* the excitement; she would let it pool up in her; but then too she'd begin to shake more and more; she'd leak over into spasmodic and oddly sad, too large movements; and she'd whimper, knowing, I suppose, that those movements were breaking the tempo in herself; again and again, tears streamed down her cheeks; she said in a not quite hoarse, in a sweet, almost hoarse whisper, "I don't want to come, Wiley, you go ahead and come."

My mind had pretty much shut off; it had become exhausted; and I didn't see how we were going to make this work; she said, "Wiley, it's all right—please, it's all right—I don't want to come."

I wondered if I should say something and try to trigger some fantasy in her; but I didn't want to risk saying something she'd find unpleasant or think was a reproach or a hint for her to be sexier. I thought if I just kept on dit-dit-ditting, sooner or later, she'd find it in herself, the trick of riding on her feelings, and getting them to rear up, crest, and topple. I held her tightly, in sympathy and pity, and maybe fear, and admiration: she was so unhysterical; she hadn't yelled at me or broken anything; she hadn't ordered me around: she was simply alone and shaking in the middle of a neural storm in her that she seemed to have no gift for handling. I said, "Orra, it's OK: I really prefer long fucks," and I went on, dit-dit-dit-dit, then I'd shift up to dit-dot, dit-dot, dit-dot, dit-dot . . . My back hurt, my legs were going; if sweat was sperm, we would have looked like liquefied snow fields.

Orra made noises, more and more quickly, and louder and louder; then the noises she made slackened off. Then, step by step, with shorter and shorter strokes, then out of control and clumsy, simply reestablishing myself inside the new approach, I settled down, fucked slowly. The prick was embedded far in her; I barely stirred; the drama of sexual movement died away, the curtains were stilled; there was only sensation on the stage.

I bumped against the stone blocks and hidden hooks that nipped and bruised me into the soft rottenness, the strange, glowing, breakable hardness of coming, of the sensations at the approaches to coming.

I panted and half-rolled and pushed and edged it in, and slid it back, sweatily—I was semi-expert, aimed, intent: sex can be like a wilderness that imprisons you: the daimons of the locality claim you: I was achingly nagged by sensations; my prick had been somewhat softened before and now it swelled with a sore-headed, but fine distension: Orra shuddered and held me cooperatively; I began to forget her.

I thought she was making herself come on the slow fucking, on the prick which, when it was seated in her like this, when I hardly moved it, seemed to belong to her as much as to me; the prick seemed to *enter* me too; we both seemed to be sliding on it, the sensation was like that; but there was the moment when I became suddenly aware of her again, of the flesh and blood and bone in my arms, beneath me. I had a feeling of grating on her, and of her grating on me. I didn't recognize the unpleasantness at first. I don't know how long it went on before I felt it as a withdrawal in her, a withdrawal that she had made, a patient and restrained horror in her, and impatience in me: our arrival at sexual shambles.

My heart filled suddenly—filled; and then all feeling ran out of it—it emptied itself.

I continued to move in her slowly, numbly, in a shabby hubbub of faceless shudderings and shufflings of the mid-section and half-thrusts, half-twitches; we went on holding each other, in silence, without slackening the intensity with which we held each other; our movements, that flopping in place, that grinding against each other, went on; neither of us protested in any way. Bad sex can be sometimes stronger and more moving than good sex. She made sobbing noises—and held on to me. After a while sex seemed very ordinary and familiar and unromantic. I started going dit-dit-dit again.

Her hips jerked up half a dozen times before it occurred to me again that she liked to thrust like a boy, that she wanted to thrust, and then it occurred to me she wanted me to thrust.

I maneuvered my ass slightly and tentatively delivered a shove, or rather, delivered an authoritative shove, but not one of great length, one that was exploratory; Orra sighed, with relief it seemed to me; and jerked, encouragingly, too late, as I was pulling back. When I delivered a second thrust, a somewhat more obvious one, more amused, almost boyish, I was like a boy whipping a fairly fast ball in a game, at a first baseman—she jerked almost wolfishly, gobbling up the extravagant power of the gesture, of the thrust; with an odd shudder of pleasure, of irresponsibility, of boyishness, I suddenly realized how physically strong Orra was, how well-knit, how well put together her body was, how great the power in it, the power of endurance in it; and a phrase—absurd and demeaning but exciting just then—came into my head: *to throw a fuck*, and I settled myself atop her, braced my toes and knees and elbows and hands on the bed and half-scramblingly worked *it*—*it* was clearly mine; but I was Orra's—worked *it* into a passionate shove, a curving stroke about a third as long as a full stroke; but amateur and gentle, that is, tentative still; and Orra screamed then; how she screamed; she made known her readiness: then the next time, she grunted: "Uhnnn-nahhhhhh . . ." a sound thick at the beginning but that trailed into refinement, into sweetness, a lingering sweetness.

It seemed to me I really wanted to fuck like this, that *I* had been waiting for this all my life. But it wasn't really my taste, that kind of fuck: I liked to throw a fuck with less force and more gradations and implications of force rather than with the actual thing; and with more immediate contact between the two sets of pleasures and with more admissions of defeat and triumph; my pleasure was a thing of me reflecting her; her spirit entering me; or perhaps it was merely a mistake, my thinking that; but it seemed shameful and automatic, naïve and animal: to throw the prick into her like that.

She took the thrust: she convulsed a little; she fluttered all over; her skin fluttered; things twitched in her, in the disorder surrounding the phallic blow in her. After two thrusts, she collapsed, went flaccid, then toughened and readied herself again, rose a bit from the bed, aimed the flattened, mysteriously funnel-like container of her lower end at me, too high, so that I had to pull her down with my hands on her butt or on her hips; and her face, when I glanced at her beneath my

lids, was fantastically pleasing, set, concentrated, busy, harassed; her body was strong, was stone, smooth stone and
wet-satin paper bags and snaky webs, thin and alive, made of
woven snakes that lived, thrown over the stone; she held the
great, writhing-skinned stone construction toward me, the bony
marvel, the half-dish of bone with its secretive; gluey-smooth
entrance, *the place where I was* — it was undefined, except for
that: *the place where I was:* she took and met each thrust —
and shuddered and collapsed and rose again: she seemed to
rise to the act of taking it; I thought she was partly mistaken,
childish, to think that the center of sex was to meet and take
the prick thrown into her as hard as it could be thrown, now
that she was excited; but there was a weird wildness, a wild
freedom, like children cavorting, uncontrolled, set free, but not
hysterical merely without restraint; the odd, thickened,
knobbed pole springing back and forth as if mounted on a web
of wide rubber bands; it was a naive and a complete release.
I whomped it in and she went, "UHNNN!" and a half-iota of
a second later, I was seated all the way in her, I jerked a minim
of an inch deeper in her, and went "UHNNN!" too. Her whole
body shook. She would go, "UHN!" And I would go, "UHN!"

Then when it seemed from her strengthening noises and
her more rapid and jerkier movements that she was near the
edge of coming, I'd start to place whomps, in neater and firmer
arrangements, more obviously in a rhythm, more businesslike,
more teasing with pauses at each end of a thrust; and that
would excite her up to a point; but then her excitement would
level off, and not go over the brink. So I would speed up: I'd
thrust harder, then harder yet, then harder and faster; she

made her noises and half-thrust back. She bit her lower lip; she set her teeth in her lower lip; blood appeared. I fucked still faster, but on a shorter stroke, almost thrumming on her, and angling my abdomen hopefully to drum on her clitoris; sometimes her body would go limp; but her cries would speed up, bird after bird flew out of her mouth while she lay limp as if I were a boxer and had destroyed her ability to move; then when the cries did not go past a certain point, when she didn't come, I'd slow and start again. I wished I'd been a great athlete, a master of movement, a woman, a lesbian, a man with a gigantic prick that would explode her into coming. I moved my hands to the corners of the mattress; and spread my legs; I braced myself with my hands and feet; and braced like that, free-handed in a way, drove into her; and the new posture, the feeling she must have had of being covered, and perhaps the difference in the thrust got to her; but Orra's body began to set up a babble, a babble of response then—I think the posture played on her mind.

But she did not come.

I moved my hands and held the dish of her hips so that she couldn't wiggle or deflect the thrust or pull away: she began to "Uhn" again but interspersed with small screams: we were like kids playing catch (her poor brutalized clitoris), playing hard hand: this was what she thought sex was; it was sexual, as throwing a ball hard is sexual; in a way, too, we were like acrobats hurling ourselves at each other, to meet in mid-air, and fall entangled to the net. It was like that.

Her mouth came open, her eyes had rolled to one side and stayed there—it felt like twilight to me—I knew where she was sexually, or thought I did. She pushed, she egged us on. She wasn't breakable this way. Orra. I wondered if she knew, it made me like her how naïve this was, this American fuck, this kids-playing-at-twilight-on-the-neighborhood-street fuck. After I seated it and wriggled a bit in her and moozed on her clitoris with my abdomen, I would draw it out not in a straight line but at some curve so that it would press against the walls of her cunt and she could keep track of where it was; and I would pause fractionally just before starting to thrust, so she could brace herself and expect it; I whomped it in and understood her with an absurd and probably unfounded sense of my sexual virtuosity; and she became silent suddenly, then she began to breathe loudly, then something in her toppled; or broke, then all at once she shuddered in a different way. It really was as if she lay on a bed of wings, as if she had a half-dozen wings folded under her, six huge wings, large, veined, throbbing, alive wings, real ones, with fleshy edges from which glittering feathers sprang backwards; and they all stirred under her.

She half-rose; and I'd hold her so she didn't fling herself around and lose her footing, or her airborneness, on the uneasy glass mountain she'd begun to ascend, the frail transparency beneath her, that was forming and growing beneath her, that seemed to me to foam with light and darkness, as if we were rising above a landscape of hedges and moonlight and shadows: a mountain, a sea that formed and grew; it grew and grew; and she said "OH!" and "OHHHH!" almost with vertigo, as if she was airborne but unsteady on the vans of her wings, and as if I was there without wings but by some magic dispensation and by some grace of familiarity; I thunked on and on, and she looked down and was frightened; the tension in her body grew vast; and suddenly a great, a really massive violence ran through her but now it was as if, in fear at her height or out of some automatism, the first of her three pairs of wings began to beat, great fans winnowingly, great wings of flesh out of which feathers grew, catching at the air, stabilizing and yet lifting her: she whistled and rustled so; she was at once so still and so violent; the great wings engendered, their movement engendered in her, patterns of flexed and crossed muscles: her arms and legs and breasts echoed or carried out the strain, or strained to move the weight of those winnowing, moving wings. Her breaths were wild but not loud and slanted every which way, irregular and new to this particular dream, and very much as if she looked down on great spaces of air; she grabbed at me, at my shoulders, but she had forgotten how to work her hands, her hands just made the gestures of grabbing, the gestures of a well-meaning, dark but beginning to be luminous, mad, amnesiac angel. She called out, "Wiley, Wiley!" but she called it out in a *whisper*, the whisper of someone floating across a night sky, of someone crazily ascending, someone who was going crazy, who was taking on the mad purity and temper of angels, someone who was tormented unendurably by this, who was unendurably frightened, whose pleasure was enormous, half-human, mad. Then she screamed in rebuke, "Wiley!" She screamed my name: *"Wiley!"*—she did it hoarsely and insanely, asking for help, but blaming me, and merely as exclamation; it was a gutter sound in part, and ugly; the ugliness, when it destroyed nothing, or maybe it had an impetus of its own, but it whisked away another covering, a membrane of ordinariness—I don't know—and her second pair of wings began to beat; her whole body was aflutter on the bed. I was as wet as—as some fish, thonking away, sweatily. Grinding away. I said, "It's OK, Orra. It's OK." And poked on. In mid-air. She shouted, *"What is this!"* She shouted it in the way a tremendously large person who can defend herself might shout at someone who was unwisely beating her up. She shouted—angrily, as in an announcement of anger, it seemed—"Oh my *God!"* Like: *Who broke this cup?* I plugged on. She raised her torso, her head, she looked me clearly in the eye, her eyes were enormous, were bulging, and she said, *"Wiley, it's happening!"* Then she lay down again and screamed for a couple of seconds. I said a little dully, grinding on, "It's OK, Orra. It's OK." I didn't want to say *Let go* or to say anything lucid because I didn't know a damn thing about female orgasm after all, and I didn't want to give her any advice and wreck things; and also I didn't want to commit myself in case this turned out to be a false alarm; and we had to go on. I pushed in, lingered, pulled back, went in, only half on beat, one-thonk-one-thonk, then one-one-one, saying, "This is sexy, this is good for me, Orra, this is very good for me," and then, "Good Orra," and she trembled in a new way at that, *"Good Orra,"* I said, *"Good . . . Orra,"* and then all at once, it happened. Something pulled her over; and something gave in; and all three pairs of wings began to beat: she was the center and the source and the victim of a storm of wing beats; we were at the top of the world; the huge bird of God's body in us hovered; the great miracle pounded on her back, pounded around us; she was straining and agonized and distraught, estranged within this corporeal-incorporeal thing, this angelic other avatar, this other substance of herself: the wings were outspread; they thundered and gaspily galloped with her; they half broke her; and she screamed, *"Wiley!"* and *"Mygodmygod"* and *"IT'S NOT STOPPING, WILEY, IT'S NOT STOPPING!"* She was pale *and* red; her hair was everywhere; her body was wet, and thrashing. It was as if something unbelievably strange and fierce—like the holy temper—lifted her to where she could not breathe or walk: she choked in the ether, a scrambling seraph, tumbling, and aflame and alien, powerful beyond belief, hideous and frightening and beautiful beyond the reach of the human. A screaming child, an angel howling in the Godly sphere: she churned without delicacy, as wild as an angel bearing threats; her body lifted from the sheets, fell back, lifted again; her hands beat on the bed; she made very loud hoarse tearing noises—I was frightened for her: this was her first time after six years of playing around with her body. It hurt her; her face looked like something made of stone, a monstrous carving; only her body was alive; her arms and legs were outspread and tensed and they beat or they were weak and fluttering. She was an angel as brilliant as a beautiful insect infinitely enlarged and irrevocably foreign: she was unlike me: she was a girl making rattling, astonished, uncontrolled, unhappy noises, a girl looking shocked and intent and harassed by the variety and viciousness of the sensations, including relief, that attacked her. I sat up on my knees and moved a little in her and stroked her breasts, with smooth sideways, winglike strokes. And she screamed, *"Wiley, I'm coming!"* and with a certain idiocy entered on her second orgasm or perhaps her third since she'd started to come a few minutes before; and we should have gone on for hours but she said, "It hurts, Wiley, I hurt, make it stop . . ." So I didn't move; I just held her thighs with my hands; and her things began to trail off, to trickle down, into little shiverings; the stoniness left her face; she calmed into moderated shudders, and then she said, she started to speak with wonder but then it became an exclamation and ended on a kind of hollow note, the prelude to a small scream: she said, "I *came* . . ." Or "I ca-a-a-ammmmmmmmme . . ." What happened was that she had another orgasm at the thought that she'd had her first.

That one was more like three little ones, diminishing in strength. When she was quieter, she was gasping, she said, "Oh you *love* me . . ."

That too excited her. When that died down, she said—angrily—"I always knew they were doing it wrong, I always knew there was nothing wrong with me . . ." And that triggered a little set of ripples. Some time earlier, without knowing it, I'd begun to cry. My tears fell on her thighs, her belly, her breasts, as I moved up, along her body, above her, to lie atop her. I wanted to hold her, my face next to hers; I wanted to hold her. I slid my arms in and under her, and she said, "Oh, Wiley," and she tried to lift her arms, but she started to shake again; then trembling anyway, she lifted her arms and hugged me with a shuddering sternness that was unmistakable; then she began to cry too.

·⟨ FREDERICK BUSCH ⟩·

Harry and Catherine

*Frederick Busch was born in Brooklyn, New York, and edu-
cated at Muhlenberg College and Columbia University. He
has written eighteen works of fiction, all of which showcase
his energy, honesty, generosity, and superbly virtuous prose
skills. This is from his 1990 novel,* Harry and Catherine, *one
of his most eloquent and deeply felt explorations of contemporary domesticity. He lives with his family in Sherborne,
New York.*

SHE WATCHED HIS EYES AS SHE DIPPED A FINGER IN HER
Calvados and touched it to her nipples. He dove to her, holding
her waist, dropping his glass, causing her to drop hers, and he
sucked the brandy, licked it, and the breast around it, and
she almost fell to her knees. She caught herself with one hand
on the brass bedpost. "Have a drink," she said, and then she
did giggle, and — she was thankful that they weren't grim, theatrical — so did Harry. But he wouldn't let her go. One arm
around her waist, still he wrested her sideways, and they fell
onto the bed, and all her brandy-applying ingenuity fell with

the brandy itself. She hadn't a thought, she thought. Neither, apparently, did he. For they had made love, before, with some invention, with an artful delaying, with cruel and delicate stallings, and with all sorts of noise. Now they were silent, and they didn't laugh any more. She lay on her back beneath him, her legs almost around him and up in the air, the calves and feet flopping as if disconnected, as Harry, with no cunning foreplay, his fingers touching only her arms and her neck, her face, and then at last her back, plunged deep into what, she was interested and grateful to know, was like a liquid core. There was little rearing and watching, no out-to-the-tip-and-slowly-back-in, as there used to be between them. It was, she thought, as if they didn't choose to separate by even that much space. Their pelvises were together, and he was deep inside her, and they rocked together not all that slowly because she couldn't wait, she didn't care if he came right now. He didn't, and neither did she, and she didn't care if they never came. Yes, she did. Yes, she did. Yes, she did.

She said his name. He panted harshly, as if he'd been running, or weeping, or both. She held him hard and moved at him selfishly, relishing the selfishness, and came—a string of firecrackers going off was what she saw, like something in the Saturday cartoons the boys had used to watch. He tightened his thighs around hers now, and squeezed her thighs together around his penis, and he groaned a deep startled sound, and Catherine came again, so hard she yelped, but she heard him. He said, *"Cath."*

Then they lay together on their sides, still locked, and then apart on their sides, him still panting, and then Harry turned toward the bright-as-daylight windows, falling into sleep as if his body knew that this would be his best night's sleep in years.

Catherine lay on her back. She touched her gluey crotch and was tempted to linger, or to wake him. And then she turned onto her side, so that her arm lay over Harry's soft chest—hard enough a couple of minutes ago, you bitch.

Now I lay me down to sleep, she thought. Thanks for the tomatoes in the pantry waiting to be washed, and the peppers and zucchini, the oregano and thyme. But I have to ask, she thought, pressing her nose and mouth into the side of his neck, its salty taste, what's supposed to happen next? To remind us for sure that we are *not* supposed to wait a long time and love long-distance and finally hop in the sack to find truth, justice, contentment, *and* measured form while living sweetly, stupidly, happily forever after?

And what happened was that she woke. Nothing saddened or disturbed her, and the falling temperatures and rising wind, the gentle, expected music of windowpanes shaken, were soothing, not unsettling. But she'd been asleep, in deep, exhausted, grateful sleep, and then she lay with her eyes open, a light sweat on her skin, and her breathing just a little fast. As if he sensed her unsettlement, Harry pulled at her. Did he know she needed comforting, or wish she did? Or was he just a great, greedy boy? He was a comforting and greedy man, she thought. But she felt that what she needed more than his needful generosity was air. She heard it outside, and she thirsted for it. And he had her pinned.

She had forgotten how Harry slept, at least how Harry slept with her. She would return to how he might sleep with whomever else, she knew. She had visited the question before. Now, though, he had reached, when she'd wakened and stirred, and had curved around her. He lay at her back and embraced her. Even in his deepest sated sleep, he reached. He lay, now, with his arm stretched over her hip and his hand cupping her abdomen, just brushing the top of her pubic hair, tickling her and stimulating her at once. She thought to wake him up, reward and punish him for turning her on, like a bright bulb in a small lamp, all heat and strange shadows thrown into corners she hadn't thought to peer at. And, on the other hand, even sexy, even languid and damp, she didn't mind being alone with Harry. The best way of being with a man, she thought sadly: alone. True? Catherine: *true?*

They Whisper

Robert Olen Butler has written seven critically acclaimed novels, including The Alleys of Eden, Sun Dance, Countrymen of Bones, On Distant Ground, *and* They Whisper, *as well as a collection of short stories,* A Good Scent from a Strange Mountain, *which won the Pulitzer Prize for fiction in 1993. He served in the U.S. Army in Vietnam as a Vietnamese linguist and a counterintelligence agent. He currently lives in Lake Charles, Louisiana, where he teaches creative writing. This excerpt was taken from* They Whisper, *perhaps his strongest work, a deeply moving novel about eroticism and sorrow.*

I WAS IN ZURICH AGAIN JUST LAST YEAR. REBECCA WASN'T there. I knew where Rebecca was and I was far away from that place. I was in Zurich and a business associate told me to go to the Utoquay, and I did. It was a floating wooden bathing pavilion on the bank of the Limmat River and it was a place where the women of Zurich went to sunbathe topless. I changed into my swimsuit and went up onto the upper deck and I strolled in this Swiss garden of nipples and it was very difficult for me to breathe, though it was a very strange place, really, like so many strange places around Europe in recent years, a place with single sunbathers, of course, but also husbands and wives together and boyfriends and girlfriends together and fellow workers together, men and women, and all the women come and they sit in the sun and they pull the tops of their suits down and their nipples are naked and there is always an air of quiet around the place, the quiet of elaborate casualness and everyone here is trying to turn nipples into elbows or wrists. There's no presumption of a secret about this place on their bodies and perhaps if you grow up with this, then it's true; if you can see a woman's nipples as readily as her knuckles or her knees, then everybody can be as rigorously nonchalant as they all seemed to be lounging on the wood planks that summer day beneath a pallid Swiss sun.

But for me, this was much too strong, all of this. For me, even a woman's elbows or wrists or knuckles or knees can knock me down with desire. So all of these nipples made me spread my towel quickly and sit on the deck because I was afraid my erection would soon pop out of my spandex suit. And I crossed my legs to hide my ardor and I leaned back on my elbows and to my left were nipples the color of brick and they seemed permanently erect, their owner apparently asleep, her forearm flung over her eyes and her brick-red nipples erect though the sun was warm, and perhaps it was her dream, perhaps her nipples were yielding in her dream to the lips of a man who loved her. And across the way a woman with nipples nearly as large as the palms of my hands was lying on her back and she put her finger in her navel and then the finger slid out and up her skin, drawing a line from her navel to her throat and then around her breast and down again and this was a very casual gesture, as idle and calm as the lapping of the water over the edge of the pavilion, and to her right were three women on their stomachs, side by side, and the bottoms of their feet were very white in the insteps but the balls of their feet and their heels and the outer rim of flesh running in between were much darker, the color of a ripe tangerine, a parenthesis of tangerine and there were these three sets of parentheses and the message spoken aside in each one was so incidental as to have disappeared, and that's what it all seemed up here, there were men scattered across the deck and they were reading newspapers or dozing or lying with their eyes shaded and a few were speaking to the women with them but their eyes never once dropped from the faces, never once acknowledged the secret tips of all these lovely breasts wrinkling into erection just below eye level or smoothing and spreading into quiescence.

And beside me to the other side was a woman who had been lying on her stomach with her face turned away when I sat down and she was very small, really, though she did not seem it at first glance because she clearly had powerful legs, not heavy with muscle but solid and strongly shaped, and now she sat up. Her hair was short and though she was not more than thirty or so, her feet were angled in sharply at the joint below the big toes and I knew these were an athlete's feet, a tumbler's feet, working feet, and though I never did find this out from her, I am certain even now that I was right, and I

could imagine her springing up to hang on rings and her triceps going hard as she pulled up and lifted these fine, working
feet and tucked them as she rose, and now that she was sitting
up beside me, her breasts seemed as strong as the rest of her,
stretching straight as if they were holding a ring pose before a
panel of judges and the nipples were prickled with bumps, as
if she'd just been told thrilling news but only her nipples really
knew about it and the gooseflesh came only here. She took an
orange from her bag and she dug both thumbs into it and a
sharp smell of the fruit brought my eyes up from her nipples
to her face and she turned her gray eyes to me and she smiled
and offered the orange. I said thank you and she took off a
section and gave it to me and we tried briefly to speak but she
spoke only Swiss German and Italian and I spoke neither and
so we shrugged at each other and I ate the orange and kissed
my fingertips and flared them before my mouth to tell her it
was good and she laughed.

We shared the orange and now it was I who was not looking
at her nipples and perhaps I understood, because it was my
glance that would be the gesture of exposure for her, but if I
could not look, then why were her breasts bare before me? If
she thought that I did not wish to look, wouldn't that make
her a little sad? This was a form of her hidden self, wasn't it?
But no longer. That had to be part of this whole thing. The
new elbows and knees. But already I was loving the angle of
her toes and the cords of her calves, so how could I not love
her nipples, and yet I was sitting here and she was feeding me
slices from the orange that she'd dug her thumbs into and I
wanted to take her thumbs into my mouth and kiss the juices

away but we could only look at each other's eyes with her nipples just a glance down.

And when the orange was finished, she turned to her bag again and took out suntan lotion and she began to rub her feet and her legs and her tummy and her arms and her breasts. She sat beside me and she rubbed her breasts and her eyes were on her work and I could look again and her nipples smoothed out a bit, though some of their soft roughness remained, and they glistened now and she smiled again at me, catching me, I think, in my stare at her breasts but she did not show any sign of that, and she lay down on her stomach and her face was turned toward me, though her eyes were closed. This was the dumbest, simplest approach of all, but I touched her arm and she opened her eyes and I motioned that I could rub lotion on her back if she wished and she nodded and said "Thank you" in heavy English and I rubbed her back and her skin was very soft though I could feel the power of her, too, beneath my hands, and as I rubbed I studied the nearly invisible fuzz that ran down the indent of her spine and I rubbed her shoulders and her arms—those lovely gymnast's triceps—and I rubbed her sturdy ribs and I brushed the sides of her breasts with my fingertips and she opened her eyes and smiled at me. And when there was nothing else obvious to cover with lotion, I put some on my fingertip and I rubbed the place behind her ear. She lifted up at this in surprise, but I pointed to the sun and frowned and touched the place again behind her ear and she laughed and she lay back down.

We did not speak again. She slept and sunned and I sat and watched her and after a while she turned onto her back and

I memorized her nipples—the iron clay red of them, the thumb and forefinger circle size of them, the little *V* gash of their tips. And this was all thrilling to me, of course. But what stirred me the most, after a time, was the rise and fall of her midriff. Her breathing seemed lovely to me. Just that, just the rise and fall of her breathing made me love her and yearn to speak with her and learn how she used this wonderful body of hers to tumble and to soar. She lay there with her breasts naked and she was breathing. She was alive. I felt a great tenderness nibbling in my own breast and I knew I would never be able to touch her but it was all right, if that was the way it was to be, because I could sit in the sunlight and watch her breathe.

"What Girls Are Made Of"

Pat Califia's books include Macho Sluts, Melting Point, The Lesbian S/M Safety Manual, *and* Doc and Fluff: The Dystopian Tale of a Girl and Her Biker. Doc and Fluff *was detained at the Canadian border and some bookstores refused to carry it because it was considered dangerous in its descriptions of violence against women. She writes about the darkly, intense side of lesbian sexuality in cool, lucid prose. This excerpt, from her short story entitled "What Girls Are Made Of," appears in* Melting Point. *Pat Califia lives in San Francisco.*

THEY STARED AT EACH OTHER FOR SEVERAL LONG SECONDS the triumphant bitch goddesses and their flustered, hijacked tourist. "Maybe she doesn't know how to eat cunt," Poison said helpfully. "Maybe she's one of those awful straight girls who gets a short haircut and hangs out in lesbian bars pretending she belongs there."

"Well?" Killer said impatiently. "What about it? Do you

know what to do with a piece of cherry pie, stud, or is your tongue just for making rude comments to your betters?"

They were not going to let her go. It was no use fighting them. Whoever would have thought that girls in lipstick and pushup bras could be so mean? "No," Bo said finally, looking at the floor. "I'll do it."

It was hard to get her tongue all the way into Killer's silky inner lips. Handcuffed to the water pipe, she couldn't get her neck to bend at the right angle. But she did her best, and Killer's flexible dancer's hips and slender legs made it easier. Out of the corner of her eye, she noticed the other women changing clothes and refreshing their makeup. Geez, if Bo was going to humiliate herself this way, the least they could do was watch.

"You're good," Killer said, tugging one of her ears. "Do it faster. Not harder, idiot—just faster!"

Killer's inner lips were thin and long, like the two halves of a razorback clam. Her teardrop-shaped clit was very small, like a seed pearl. She seemed to like having Bo's tongue go around it without actually touching it. The thought of biting her was very tempting but then she'd probably stay handcuffed to this pipe until she starved to death.

"Oh, yes, that's it. Do that!" Killer said, squeezing Bo's head. There was a knock on the dressing room door. One of the other girls told somebody they'd be right out. Killer came silently, biting her own hand. Bo was shaken by the sexual electricity that passed through her own body when Killer peaked. She barely noticed the dancers filing out and shutting the door behind them. They had left one of her hands free. It was the wrong hand, but nothing else was in sight. Wait—there was Poison's vibrator. She'd left it on the floor. Bo had to strain to reach it with her boot toes, but she managed to nudge it within reach.

There was no way she could come sitting down with her pants on. Bo somehow managed to pry her boots off, undo the jeans with one hand, and wiggle out of them. Lucky she didn't believe in underwear. She closed her eyes and tried to remember the exact shape of Killer's clit, the way her palms fit over Bo's ears, the other girls breathing faster as Killer got more excited, how she couldn't escape, couldn't get away, and had no idea what would happen next.

The awkward fingers of her left hand kept rebelling and cramping up. Frustrated, Bo switched the vibrator on and held it against her outer lips. She was embarrassed to even touch the thing. She had seen them in porn shops often enough, in boxes that always had these dopey pictures of women running them over their faces. It felt good, but it kept getting caught in her pubic hair. She tried to point it at her clit, but she was so wet that the head of it somehow slipped down and went into her. It seemed content to stay there, purring away, while Bo stroked her clit.

It just wasn't enough. She needed more, something any-thing to push herself over the edge! She stared around the room, wild-eyed. Right by her left thigh was another love of-fering from Poison, the discarded pair of tit clamps. Bo could sometimes make herself come just by twisting her own nipples. It was hard to get them on one-handed. Her nipples kept wanting to slip out of the clips. But finally she got both sides to catch.

Oh, God, she was going to come. It was inevitable. Even if the building blew up or her hands fell off, so much pressure had accumulated, Bo knew she would explode. She didn't have Killer's self-control. She heard herself whining panting and then saying, "Please, Please."

The door opened and Killer walked in. "Yes, you may," Killer said, and jammed her high-heeled shoe between Bo's legs, pinning her hand and the vibrator in place. Bo came with the sharp heel of the dancer's shoe against her perineum. "Come again," Killer said, and jerked on the chain that connected the clamps. She also rocked her heel into Bo's tender flesh. And Bo came again, in terror and shock. "Still want to call the cops?" Killer asked. "No, I didn't think so. Stick around. Pets always get smarter when you play with them."

"Good boy," Crash said, replacing Killer in front of Bo. "Now it's my turn to ride the pony."

Bo guessed it was kind of stupid, but she'd never really noticed before that women liked to come in so many different ways. Crash had coarse pubic hair that made her face burn. Instead of Killer's elegant Art Deco genital geometry, her cunt was built like a '50s diner. It was robust, with shorter, thicker inner lips. The head of her clit was perfectly round and the size of a pencil eraser. She didn't get wet as quickly as Killer. She wanted a lot of long, slow, light strokes with a teasing little flutter at the end. Nobody told Bo that she couldn't, so she kept masturbating while she tried to get Crash to come. For some reason, she kept thinking about the short porn clip she'd seen in the video booth. Was this exactly like that woman sucking cock, or was it completely different? Probably both, Bo decided, though she couldn't have explained why. She was too busy jamming her face into Crash's thighs, sucking her clit like it was a straw buried in a milkshake. The dancer had finally gotten really juicy, and Bo was afraid she'd have to go back onstage before she got off. Finally Crash started pulling her hair—quite a trick, since Bo's flattop was less than an inch long—and tilted her pelvis so Bo's tongue was moving in and out of her cunt. "Yesyesyes," she sang. "Good dog, good dog, good dog" and finally, "Sweet Jesus, yes, good boy!"

-⟨ MARY CAPONEGRO ⟩-

"The Star Cafe"

*Few writers young or old take as many chances as Mary Ca-
ponegro. Challenging and innovative, she consistently explores and expands the boundaries of short fiction. Her work
is a daringly original synthesis of the lyric, the cerebral, and
the erotic. She has taught creative writing and literature at
Brown University, Rhode Island School of Design, and the
Institute of American Indian Arts in Santa Fe, New Mexico.
Her short fiction has appeared in literary journals, including
Fiction International, Sulfer and Mississippi Review. Caponegro is the winner of the 1988 General Electric Younger
Writers Award and the 1991 Rome Prize for literature. Born
in 1956, she lives in the Finger Lakes region of New York
where she is assistant professor of English at Hobart and Wil-
liam Smith Colleges.*

"YOU'RE BEING CRYPTIC AGAIN," SHE SAID. "YOU'RE TRYING
to confuse me. And I need the ladies' room, does that ring a
bell? I may as well tell you that it's illegal not to have one in
a public eating place, so don't try to tell me there isn't any."

"You think you're so smart," he raised his voice to match hers. "I have something to tell you too. There is, technically speaking, no ladies' room. There is, however, one rest room, androgynous, past the bar and to your right."

She began the journey immediately. When she'd taken only a few steps he called to her, by name, for the first time since that very first time.

"Carol!"

She turned around.

"We're through."

That was fine with her; she turned away again directly and continued on the prescribed route. Once through a corridor she found the door immediately to her right, marked simply "rest." She opened it, entered, and shut it behind her, pushing in the little circle in the middle of the knob to lock it, then tried to jiggle the knob to make sure. She realized how silly that was; who was she locking out? The man who had seen and known her body to the full extent of possibility between human beings? But locking it made her feel better. The interior was clean enough, she would have tried to hold out if it hadn't been. This bathroom was extremely clean, in fact, so she didn't feel the need to get in and out as quickly as possible. It was mirrored, of course, mirrored tiles on the walls and floor. Also the ceiling. The toilet and sink were ordinary. A fresh bar of soap lay in the dish on the arm of the sink—so much nicer than powdery stuff out of a dispenser, she thought. How good it would feel to have clean hands. She rubbed the soap between her palms for a long time, working up a rich lather with warm water from the faucet. She decided to wash her face as well; she hadn't had the opportunity in so long. She held her hair with one hand but couldn't completely avoid getting it wet. She didn't mind; she would happily have dunked her whole head into the basin for the feel of this welcome refreshment.

In fact, why stop there, she thought, and pulled her blouse off over her head. She felt sweaty and horrible; scrubbing some soap under her arms would make her feel a little better, since she couldn't shower. She unhooked the closure in front of her bra and slipped the straps down her arms one at a time with her wet hand. In the mirror she stared at her small breasts, and was pleased with them. Her nipples were hard. She rubbed the soap vigorously under her arms, then rinsed, trying to stand over the sink in such a way that the least water would spill on the floor.

She had forgotten to check for a towel before she started; there was none, so she dabbed herself dry with pieces of toilet paper. She'd almost forgotten about her urgency; she'd make some superficial attempt at washing of genitalia after. She pulled down her panties, stepped out of them and hung them on a hook she'd just noticed protruding from the door. She rescued her blouse from where it had fallen and hung that too. She gathered up her skirt with her right hand, intending to sit on the toilet, but was distracted by suddenly seeing herself in the mirrored wall, as if seeing another person. She looked at this person who held her skirt in her arms so that it draped her hips but revealed her belly, fur and thighs. Her breasts were still uncovered also, and just as she had found them adequate, satisfying, she now found this lower region of

her body, in fact the whole body, cut off as it was at the waist —
she found the entire image attractive.

She stood transfixed by this lovely landscape under canopy
of skirt. Her flesh seemed firmer than she remembered, more
muscle tone; maybe the exercises she'd been doing in the
morning and before bedtime had finally paid off. It had been
hard to motivate herself to do them, with no prospect of anyone to appreciate the results, since she'd had no way of knowing about the cafe owner. She couldn't have predicted that,
though as it was happening, there had been, in the midst of
all that anguish and terror and pleasure, a tiny seed of déjà
vu; that was a common phenomenon, of course.

Well, it didn't make much difference in the end, did it?
She knew that she often allowed herself to become the victim
of her own speculations, reflections. Now it all seemed un-
important compared to the immediacy of the woman in the
mirror, the urgency of that woman's sexuality or physicality.
Strange to feel genuinely aroused by this image of herself. She
amused herself with the idea that it was perfectly logical for
her to associate her unaccompanied reflection with arousal,
since that had been the consistent image during her definitive
sexual experience.

Now the woman in the mirror was touching herself, sliding
her palm up her thigh, transferring the skirt to the guardian-
ship of the left hand. Then she left skin to approach her
breasts. She caressed them fervently, then left skin again to
return below the skirt, lingering for a long time when the hand
met flesh again, languidly rubbing the soft pubic hair, just a
shade darker than the honey-colored hair of her head, which

fell away from her shoulders, skimming the floor as she bent low for the mirror.

The mirror-woman did a seductive dance, holding the skirt tight across her hips, swaying, she watched the curve of her calves as she gracefully inscribed the area of the bathroom floor, often lifting her leg so high that her lips were visible.

She was extremely aroused by this time, and not ashamed of it, she wanted to possess this beautiful moving image. She felt a fullness in her groin, decided it was her old need to urinate, which seemed less and less urgent, she couldn't be bothered with addressing that now — it was confusing how similar that feeling was with that of being sexually excited. She was rubbing herself, much more vigorously than was her habit; she let the skirt drop to have both hands. She tried to put one finger of her free hand inside herself but couldn't gain entry, despite the fact that she was very wet by now. It wasn't necessary anyway, and she was happy enough to have access to both hands for rubbing.

She was so tensed and excited that her vision was blurred; she'd lost the mirror's reflection, but it was firmly fixed in her mind; she dwelled on all the postures, the confronting gaze, the beauty and sensuality of that body. She needed some kind of support, weak from so much excitement. When leaning against the sink proved insufficient she quickly closed the lid of the toilet and sat there.

Under the skirt she rubbed so fast that her hand was tiring, so she supported the right with the left, cupped the two and stroked, leaning back against the tank. She recalled there must be semen in her still, if he had come, that is, but he must have come, at least once, and probably generously, he had to have, it just wasn't possible—she felt it coming out of her, not just dribbling but in spurts, as she herself climaxed. She cried out with the new pleasure of it, an intense, confined pleasure, as she felt suddenly claustrophobic; she needed air, even if it was just the air of the corridor. She rose and unlocked the door by turning the knob hard, opened it and stuck her head out, like a seasick traveler leaning out a porthole she saw down the length of the corridor into the room with the bar, where it had all begun. Directly in the line of her vision was the poster of Greece; it was far away, and the contents of the little boxes were fuzzy, like the last letters of the eye-doctor's chart, but she could see rocks and white sand, and tall, white columns. She was drawn toward them, she wanted to see every box clearly; her nakedness did not inhibit her for some reason. He didn't matter so much anymore; she wouldn't let him keep her from exploring. There was nothing to be embarrassed about. No one was there.

⋅⋚ MICHAEL CHABON ⋛⋅

The Mysteries
of Pittsburgh

Michael Chabon received his B.A. from the University of Pittsburgh and his M.F.A. from the University of California at Irvine. He is the author of two novels, The Mysteries of Pittsburgh *and* Wonder Boys, *and a short story collection,* A Model World and Other Stories. *His work is characterized by its highly evocative, intelligent lyricism and ranges from the bitingly satirical to the deeply poignant. This passage is from* The Mysteries of Pittsburgh. *Michael Chabon lives in Los Angeles with his wife and daughter.*

WHEN WE WENT TO BED THAT NIGHT IT WAS LOUD AND FAST again, again she took control, and I found myself, inevitably perhaps, crouching on my elbows and knees—that way; I twisted and buried my face. She said, then, in an odd, clear voice which cut through everything, that she wished she could fuck me, that there must be a way, and something very primitive deep inside me awoke with a start. I rolled over, panting, but came to a definite halt. Phlox began to sob, and I wondered, unclenching my fists, if she was crying because the thing she'd wished for had frightened her, or because she could not have it, or if it was because she knew, now, that she could have it, because somehow I had been changed.

"I didn't mean it," she said, tumbling over onto the bed.

"All right," I said. I knelt beside her, ran my fingers through her faded hair. I said things that I forgot as soon as I said them. In ten minutes we were going at it again, and although I'd wanted it to be more gentle this time, had wanted to embrace, to linger, in no time at all it was exactly like wrestling; we bit and exclaimed, and I found myself twisting her into the pose I'd held just a little while before. I stared all the way down her glistening back to the tangle of her distant head.

"Can I?" I said.

"Do you want to?"

"Can I?"

"Yes," she said. "You'd better. Now."

I went to her cluttered vanity and scooped out a dollop of cold petroleum jelly, prepared everything Arthur had trained me so well to prepare, but immediately on entering that pinched, plain orifice of so little character, I lost heart, because I simply could not understand what I was about to do; it was neither backward nor forward, or else it was both at the same time, but it was too confusing for me to desire it anymore, and I said, "It's all a mistake."

"It is not," she said. "Go, ah! go. Slow, baby."

When we were through, and we'd collapsed, she said that it had hurt and it had felt all right, that it was frightening as sex could be, and I said that I knew it. We stopped talking. I felt her grow heavy, heard the slow gathering of her breath. I slipped out of bed and went to find my clothes. Dressing furtively in the darkness, pulling on each sock, I felt very happy, for one instant, as though I were rising at three in the morning for a fishing trip, and there were sandwiches and apples to be packed away. I decided not to leave a note.

"Lyricism"

Charles D'Ambrosio's short stories are richly textured and deeply thoughtful tales of American heartbreak and American grace. His best work is a masterful combining of the bleak and the beautiful. This excerpt is from his story "Lyricism."

JOAN ALWAYS WORE HER HAIR IN A PONYTAIL, KNOTTED WITH green rubber bands, or bits of yarn, or sometimes clipped back with barrettes or bobby pins. But on one of Potter's visits, she wore it tied with a black velvet ribbon. The ribbon seemed prissy for Joan, who was rough, and something of a tomboy, and Potter told her so. They had slipped between the barbed wire and were walking through the pasture. It was early fall, he remembered, and he heard killdeers crying, and cattails rustled along the creek, and clusters of goldenrod and purple loosestrife bloomed across the field. The grass was dry and flaxen, and when the wind swept across it, shifting patterns of light and dark moved like ocean swells through the field.

The ribbon she wore was so queer, so unusual, Potter made fun of it, and Joan shoved him, and ran away, leaping up to see over the waves of tall grass. Potter chased after her, and finally pulled her down, and they lay together in a bed of trampled grass, silent but breathing so heavily that Potter was embarrassed. It was strange, hearing a girl breathe. They were quiet for some time. Potter remembered listening to the wet sound of their breathing and the wind and the sough like surf rolling over the grass and watching a skein of Canadian honkers wedge through the gray sky above them. It was like being underwater, silent and slow that way. "If you don't like my ribbon, you could take it off," Joan said. Potter didn't say anything, and Joan sat up on her knees, her back facing him. Potter looked at the black ribbon, tied in a bow. "Yeah, go ahead," Joan said. Her hair had shafts of straw sticking to it. Potter reached up and touched the bow. The ribbon was soft and had a smooth gloss, a sort of sheen, when you rubbed it one way, but it was stiff and dull if you rubbed it the other way. His hand skimmed the arrows of feathery, dark hair along the back of her neck as he untied the bow. Her hair fell loose. She shook it free and the straw flew from it and she turned around. "My mother said it would look nice," she said. Potter held the strip of velvet, rubbing his thumb back and forth, feeling first the smooth way, then the stiff way. Then he leaned forward and saw her close her eyes, so he closed his too. Her kiss was the quietest thing in the world. Potter never wanted to open his eyes again, but he did, after a while, and Joan was looking at his face, and smiling. "My sister taught me how in the mirror," she said. Potter couldn't say anything at all. He just leaned forward for more, and he felt the lavender of her lips, and then something else, the moist pink slip of her tongue. He jumped up and started off across the field waving the black velvet ribbon like a flag fluttering in the evening air.

During the chase, sometime before Joan caught and wrestled him to the ground, Potter dropped the ribbon, and though they looked everywhere, trying to be thorough, they never found it. He apologized to Joan over and over as they walked in the falling dark to the warm yellow light of Joan's house. He imagined Mrs. Vitulli would wonder what happened to the ribbon, and he imagined she would find out. He said goodbye to Joan and waited until the door closed. Then he ran back into the field alone and searched for the ribbon until it was too dark to see and far too silent and dark to pretend he wasn't scared. He'd begun to imagine, not a winding black ribbon, but snakes sliding through the dark grass, and he was almost too afraid to move but he forced himself, even though the fear stayed with him as he climbed the clear-cut in absolute darkness, hearing the wires hum. The fear followed him all the way home, as he imagined the lost ribbon lying in the grass.

Players

It has taken Don DeLillo some ten novels and a perserver-ing dedication to make his voice heard, but that voice has become virtually emblematic of the manic end of a manic (not to say lunatic) century. Casually tossing around sub-jects like death, sex, murder, particle physics, college foot-ball, political assassination, hate crimes, industrial accidents, sensory overload, and mass destruction, DeLillo has captured a basic truth of the times, which is that we really don't know what we're doing or what is going on around us. He was born in 1936 and has won many major literary awards, and he is regarded a stylist without peer (or without many), but it is the dark recesses that he is exploring, and one thing about dark recesses is that you never know what you are likely to find.

THE BEDROOM WAS FAIRLY DARK, GETTING ONLY INDIRECT light. He thought her gravely beautiful, nude. She touched his arm and he recalled a moment in the car when she'd put her hands to his face, bottles hitting the pavement, and the strangeness he felt, the angular force of their differences. Nothing about them was the same or shared. Age, experience, wishes, dreams. They were each other's stark surprise, their histories nowhere coinciding. Lyle realized that until now he hadn't fully understood the critical nature of his involvement, its grievousness. Marina's alien reality, the secrets he would never know, made him see this venture as something more than a speculation.

She had a thick waist, breasts set wide apart. Bulky over all, lacking deft lines, her legs solid, she had a sculptural power about her, an immobile beauty that made him feel oddly in-adequate — his leanness, fair skin. It wasn't just the remote tenor of her personality, then, that brought him to the visible edge of what he'd helped assemble, to the pressures and con-sequences. Her body spoke as well. It was a mystery to him, how these breasts, the juncture of these bared legs, could make him feel more deeply implicated in some plot. Her body was "meaningful" somehow. It had a static intensity, a "serious-ness" that Lyle could not interpret. Marina nude. Against this standard, everything else was bland streamlining, a collection of centerfolds, assembly line sylphs shedding their bralettes and teddy pants.

They were both standing, the bed between them. Light from the air shaft, a stray glare, brought a moment of definition to her strong, clear face. She was obviously aware of the contem-plative interest she'd aroused in him. She put her hands to her breasts, misunderstanding. Not that it mattered. Her body would never be wrong, inexplicable as it was, a body that assimilated his failure to understand it. He nourished her by negative increments. A trick of existence.

She knelt on the edge of the bed. He watched the still divisions her eyes appeared to contain, secret reproductions of Marina herself. He tried helplessly to imagine what she saw, as though to bring to light a presiding truth about himself, some vast assertion of his worth, knowledge accessible only to women whose grammar eluded him. The instant she glanced at his genitals he felt an erection commence.

In bed he remembered the man on the roof. Such things are funny. Trapped in the act of having sex. It exposes one's secret feeling of being involved in something comically shameful. Luis in the doorway with a pump-action shotgun. It's funny. It exposes one's helplessness. He wondered what "pump-action" meant and why he'd thought of it and whether it had multi-level significance.

All this time they were making love. Marina was spacious, psychologically, an elaborate settling presence. At first she moved easily, drawing him in, unwinding him, a steadily deepening concentration of resources, gripping him, segments, small parts, bits of him, dashes and tads. She measured his predispositions. She even struggled a little, attaching him to his own body. How this took place he couldn't have said exactly. Marina seemed to know him. Her eyes were instruments of incredibly knowing softness. At her imperceptible urging he felt himself descend, he felt himself occupy his body. It made such sense, every pelvic stress, the slightest readjustment of some fraction of an inch of flesh. He braced himself, listening to the noises, small clicks and strains, the moist slop of their pectorals in contact. When it ended, massively, in a great shoaling transit, a leap of decompressing force, they whispered in each other's ear, wordlessly, breathing odors and raw heat, small gusts of love.

⋅{ E. L. DOCTOROW }⋅

Billy Bathgate

*To read E. L. Doctorow is to be dazzled and exhilarated by
the power of art. He is a master storyteller with a unique
voice and profound vision. His novels are richly evocative,
lyrically impassioned, and stunningly sophisticated retellings
of American history. A Kenyon product, Doctorow has experimented with many literary forms—the western, science fiction, the political novel, the crime novel. Bursting into the
popular consciousness with the period piece* Ragtime, *he often
seems intoxicated and bedazzled by the personal richness of
American history.* Billy Bathgate, *a gangster novel published
in 1989, was made into a movie, a process that Doctorow
(among others) has turned into a confirmatory event (the way
being published in paperback used to be viewed).*

MUCH LATER REBECCA AND I WERE SITTING ON ONE OF THE
couches and she had her legs crossed at the knees and one
dirty foot swinging and her nightgown showing below the hem
of her black lace dress. She was the last kid there. She raised
her arms and she pulled her black hair back behind her head

and did something deft back there the way girls do with their hair so that it stays the way they fix it without any visible reason to and despite the law of gravity. Maybe I was a little drunk by then, maybe we both were. Also the dancing had been warm and close. I was smoking a cigarette and she took it out of my fingers and drew on it, one puff, and blew out the smoke without inhaling and put the cigarette back in my fingers. I saw now she was wearing mascara on her eyelashes and eyelids and had on that communal red lipstick, paled somewhat since its application, and was glancing at me sideways with her foot swinging, and those eyes dark as black grapes, and her white neck draped in that torn shawl of dusty pink—I had no warning or preparation from one moment to the next, I was swimming in a realm of intimacy, as if I had just met her, or as if I had just lost her, but surely as if I had never roof-fucked her. My mouth went dry she was so incredibly childishly beautiful. Until this moment I had been the party-giver and big boss of the evening, dispensing his largesse and granting his favors. All those dances—oh I knew everyone knew I favored her on my randy forays up the fire escape, but it was athletics, I paid her, for christsake, I must have been staring at her because she turned away and lowered her eyes, her foot going madly—all those dances I had danced with her and only her were the exacting ceremonies of possession. And this ancient witch child understood before I did that everything was now up in the heart, as if my rise in the world had lifted us to an immensity of consequence, which we were now allowed to see, like a distance ahead of us, like a horizon. They must all have understood, every fucking kid there, while I thought what I had been feeling was only a sweetly mellow good time.

So when everyone else had gone we lay for the first time together without any clothes on that same couch, everyone else asleep, even Garbage in some inner bin of his privacy. We lay in the dark cellar of dust and ash, and I was passive and on my back and Rebecca lay on top of me and cleaved herself on me letting herself down with a long intake of her breath which I felt as a cool flute of air on my neck, and slowly awkwardly she learned her rhythm upon me as I was patient to allow her to do. My hands were on her back for a while and then on her buttocks, I followed the soft down with my fingers, I knew it was as black as her hair, it went from the bottom of her spine down into the crack between her ass, and then I put my finger on her small ring of an asshole and as she raised her hips I touched it, and as she lowered her hips I lost it in the clamp of her hard buttocks. Her hair fell forward as she raised herself and it brushed my face, and when she lowered herself it fell around my ears, and I kissed her cheeks as she rested and I felt her lips on my neck and her hard little nipples against my chest and her wet thighs on my thighs, and then I didn't remember when it started she was making little discoveries which she voiced in private almost soundless whimperings in my ear and then she moved into some arrhythmic panic and went stiff and I felt around my cock the grasp of her inner musculature and when I reached down with my finger and touched the asshole it clamped around my fingertip and released and contracted and released in the same rhythm as her interior self was squeezing and unsqueezing my cock and I couldn't stand it anymore I arched myself into her and pulled back, raising myself and lowering myself with her dead bodyweight as vehemently as if I were on top, pretty soon going so fast she was being bounced on my chest and thighs with little grunts until she found my rhythm and went stuttering and imperfectly and finally workingly, smoothly against it, meeting me when I was to be met, leaving me when I was leaving to be left, and that was so unendurably exquisite I shot into her and held her down against me with my hands while I came pulsing up into her milkingly lovely little being as far as I could go. And she held her arms around me to get me through that, and then there was peace between us, and we lay as we were with such great trust as to require no words or kisses, but only the gentlest slowest and most coordinate drift into sleep.

-·{ PAM DURBAN }·-

"World of Women"

Pam Durban is the author of a short story collection, All Set
About with Fever Trees, *and a novel,* The Laughing Place.
*She writes about familial love and familial lies with intelli-
gence, elegance, tenderness, and generosity. This excerpt from
the short story "World of Women" illustrates her graceful lyricism.*

THERE WILL COME A TIME, YEARS LATER, WHEN A WOMAN
will touch him and pull him under, back to this night, and it
will all come back to him—the panic first, the gulping, gasping feel of panic, then jubilation, freedom, then something
else that he had forgotten. They will be lying in a room in his
basement apartment with the window open and the rain steady
on the earth and a thick blue stub of candle burning beside
the mattress, the kind of light he likes for lovemaking, for the
way it quickens and subsides, for the mystery it makes of faces
and bodies.

As she moves under him and he moves with her, he will
feel panic begin to rise, shutting off his air, and spread out

through his body until he feels himself disappearing, unable to move, unable to breathe or pull. He will struggle up to try and see her face, to find himself again, but she will pull him down, the candle flame will rock shadows all over the room. She will pull until he lets go as he's learned to do, to the rocking that he recognizes now as the rocking of trees against the starlight, the tight look of buds along limbs, the lost star at the center of himself around which everything tightened, and all, every one, is desire and he gives himself over to it. Until she opens out in front of him, opens, then closes again and he opens like a gill, a hungry mouth, and just at the moment when he feels himself so deep inside her he is nothing but this rocking and swaying, he feels a shift, a stir, and though she holds him there, wants and keeps him there, he feels himself pushed out, rocked free, wave after wave carrying him out, away.

They will lie apart then, touching, and when he feels lonely again for that place where he lost himself, he will haul himself back on top of her and watch her face. He will lift the fine strands of hair that are stuck to her forehead, one by one. He will touch and hold each breast while she strokes him up and down his back, smiling up at him and watching through those Egyptian-dark eyes, and he will start to talk. He will try and tell her everything, everything he knows about how it feels to be taken in and then set free. He will clench and unclench his fist to show her what he means when he talks about entering and leaving this world where men come and go. He will talk about how you leave only to enter again and always into the same world so that no leaving is ever final or free.

And then his voice will slow, and then it will stop because she has a held hand over his mouth, a soft hand, sharp with salt. She will press her hips up against him, say "Sssh, don't talk," and he will enter her and feel himself drawn back toward that place again before he can say what he wants to say, what he never gets to say, before he can tell somebody that the world where women live has no end, it is round, it has only beginnings and everything comes back to the place where it began.

He will groan then, and press his face into the warm hollow of her shoulder and neck, and see himself again in the pool that night a long time ago, paddling back toward Sara and feeling that longing, that loneliness for his old floundering, helpless self, the one lifted out again and again, the one held close. And he will hold to her then and press his face deeper into her neck, under her hair, and with his eyes shut tight, he will see his shadow beneath him on the floor of the pool and remember how cold it looked, cold and far away.

JENNIFER EGAN

The Invisible Circus

Jennifer Egan is the author of a novel, The Invisible Circus, *and a collection of short stories,* The Emerald City. *Haunting, heartbreaking, mesmerizing, and spellbinding are words frequently used to describe her work. Her prose, luminous and lustrous, has the uncanny ability to suggest poignant silences.*

OUTSIDE, SIESTA HOUR HAD FALLEN. THE SHUTTERS WERE down. Phoebe could think of nothing but lying down with Wolf; the meal, the wine, even the conflict between them had quickened it. As the craving sharpened, it nagged, distracting her from everything but the beat of Wolf's footsteps beside her. How long would it be before they were back in their room? Hours, Phoebe thought, hours and hours, and the knowledge nearly brought her to tears. She began torturing herself with memories of them together, yesterday, this morning, and a demented sort of clarity descended upon her. Nothing mattered but that, having it back. To hell with Carla and everything else.

At a cul-de-sac they stopped. Wolf shut his eyes, kissing

Phoebe as if to pull something from within her, deeper than her mouth or throat—from her lungs, heart, stomach. Overhead Phoebe glimpsed tall houses with their green shutters closed. She and Wolf were trembling, even their mouths shook. She wished she were wearing a skirt like that other day. This was torture, like needing desperately to pee and being stranded; once she'd lost a pair of skis that way, left them lying in the snow, and when she came back from the bathroom, they were gone. Afterward she'd lied about it, said someone broke her lock while she was eating lunch. Her own desperation had shamed her. Now her hips were wedged against Wolf's. When Phoebe kissed his neck, he leapt as if she'd shocked him. "Let's get a room," he said.

They'd passed a hotel before lunch. They made for this now, unsmiling, like two thieves who must reach a window before an alarm goes off.

Wolf made the arrangements and they sprang up the marble stairs to the room. It was a fancy hotel. Wolf had trouble with the key but the door finally opened. Phoebe caught a blur of velvet and gold as they made for the bed, but the shades were drawn. The moment they were naked she took Wolf into her mouth, something she hadn't dared try because it scared her—there seemed a danger of choking or damage to the throat but now that very fear egged her on, she wanted something more. Phoebe shut her eyes, taking long slow pulls. Wolf lay very still beneath her. After each breath he would wait a long time before taking another, until suddenly he shuddered, crying out so violently that Phoebe was certain she'd damaged him—she pulled away, her mouth filled with a very strong taste, not bad exactly but strong, too strong; she swallowed quickly to be rid of it. But the taste stayed in her mouth, and for some reason Phoebe began to cry and stretched beside Wolf, sobbing. He lay like a corpse. When finally Phoebe looked at him she saw tears running from the corners of his eyes, a steady flow like something leaking accidentally from inside him. His chest shook when he breathed, but he kept his eyes closed and said nothing. They lay that way for some time. There was a feeling in the air of hopelessness. Yet even now, even amidst that hopelessness, Phoebe still wanted more; she was two people, one despairing, the other greedy and low, overjoyed when Wolf roused himself and moved down to stroke her with his mouth—the sensations were murderous, unbearable, she came almost instantly, like being smacked in the head and losing consciousness. Afterward she lay as if broken, the words "sickness unto death" drifting through her mind from someplace; she was drifting free of everything now, even Wolf. Thank God for these moments of calm, although they never lasted long enough; soon the inevitable pounding started up again like a toothache, faintly at first but mounting steadily until she and Wolf clung to each other and he pushed himself inside her, both of them gasping slightly at the rawness of their flesh.

Afterward they lay flung together. The bedspread smelled of orange peels. Phoebe wondered if there was a potpourri somewhere.

"This is bad," Wolf said without strength. Phoebe nodded. She felt as if someone else had abused them, a reckless, insatiable third party.

"I feel crazy," Wolf said, his voice flat. "I swear to God."

Phoebe looked at the room. It was full of shadows.

"I love you," Wolf said. "I love you, Phoebe." He'd never said this before, although Phoebe had said it to him, many times. He was watching her with a slightly crazy look, yet at the same time he seemed attentive to something else, like a noise in the hallway. Phoebe listened, but heard only the vague beginnings of that pounding deep within herself, like evil footsteps making their approach, and it frightened her now, her whole body hurt and she didn't want any more but she did; some part of her was always empty.

"I love you," Wolf said, between kisses. "Phoebe, I love you." They moved together sorrowfully, with apology almost, like strangers consoling each other in the midst of a crisis.

A drenching sleep overcame them. When they woke, it was well past dark. The day had gone, leaving Phoebe with a panicky sense of having missed something important. They discussed whether to drive back now, in darkness, or wait until morning. The prospect of a long drive at this hour was dismal, but even more dismal was the thought of remaining overnight without toothbrushes or changes of clothes. A mood of failure hung in the room like a smell. Phoebe was anxious to confine it within the present day, keep it from touching tomorrow.

They would go back, they decided. Back to their home, such as it was. Moroccan tiles glazed the bathroom. Big soft towels were folded over rods. "How much does this place cost?" Phoebe asked.

"The beauty of credit cards," Wolf said. "I have no idea."

"We're paying for the whole night, aren't we?" she said. "Even if we leave."

Wolf smiled haggardly. "I'd say we've gotten our money's worth."

In the shower they gently soaped each other's bodies, but despite their halfhearted efforts to resist, were soon hunched against the tiles, hot water beating against them. Wolf looked paler than Phoebe had ever seen him. She wondered if losing too much semen could be physically dangerous, but decided it was not the time to ask.

A towel at his waist, Wolf examined his beard in the mirror above the sink. He'd been shaving twice each day so his stubble wouldn't hurt her, and so much shaving had made a rash on his neck. Watching him, Phoebe was startled by the look Wolf exchanged with himself: a cold mix of regret and stubbornness, the look of a man who believes he has ruined his life. But when his gaze met Phoebe's, she saw the tenderness again, that helpless opening which seemed to flush away everything else. "Let me dry you," he said, and did so very gently, tamping Phoebe's shoulders and breasts as if wiping sweat from a feverish child.

In the bedroom they switched on a light. The room was beautiful. Their failure to make proper use of it dogged Phoebe. Clothing lay everywhere, though the bed looked surprisingly neat.

"All right," Wolf said, checking to see they'd left nothing behind. "We're doing okay here."

The night was cool and clear, moonless. The only illumination on the empty road came from the sweep of their headlights. To Phoebe the glittery sky had a hapless, random look, as if some precious substance had been wasted there.

ARC d'X

Steve Erickson, who writes film criticism for L.A Weekly, *is the author of five novels,* Days Between Stations, Rubicon Beach, Tours of the Black Clock, Leap Year, *and* ARC d'X. *He is a boldly imaginative and totally original explorer of history's dark nights, which he recounts with a fierce, passionate momentum. This selection is from* ARC d'X, *a daring and bizarre work (based on the life of Thomas Jefferson's mulatto lover, Sally Hemmings) about the varied incarnations of an eighteenth-century slave.*

BEYOND THE LOBBY WAS A BAR THAT HADN'T BEEN OCCUPIED in years; the stairs were to the left. Georgie went up the stairs floor by floor. He went down each shadowy unlit corridor looking for room twenty-eight until he found it near the back of the hotel, where it occurred to him for the first time that he had no idea what he was doing. He knocked so halfheartedly he could barely hear the knock himself. He slowly turned the doorknob and found it unlocked.

For several moments he stood in the open doorway staring

into a pitch-black room. He searched the wall next to him for a light but the switch wasn't there. At first he thought the room was empty but then he knew it wasn't empty; he knew some- one was close by and he felt the dark of the room challenging him, he felt the night challenging him as though there was one more thing for him to prove. He was inside the room with the door partly but not altogether closed behind him and was surprised how quickly she was suddenly there next to him; all he saw of her was, very dimly, the arm that shot out of the dark to push the door closed. Then he heard her breathing and smelled her hair. He waited for her to say something and wondered what he would answer. He waited for her to turn on the light. He felt her surprise when the tips of her fingers brushed his bare chest; they flinched as though singed by the flames of his tattooed belly. But then her fingers returned to him. He felt them fumble toward his neck to confirm the chain with its tag. She grabbed the chain and pulled him forward into the room until he stumbled against the bed. Though he now understood there wasn't going to be any light, he still waited for her to say something, and then he under- stood there wasn't going to be anything said. For a moment he was confused, wondering where she was in the dark, until he realized she was on the bed that he stood alongside. Lying at its edge, she unbuttoned his pants and freed him and put him in her mouth. He touched her long hair and her breasts in consternation.

Her breasts felt big to him but he couldn't be sure, since he'd never felt a woman's breasts. Even if he might have been able to construct a mental picture of the woman who lay before him, even if—like a blind man listening to descriptions of colors he's never seen—he wasn't utterly without reference points in the touch of a woman's breast, he would have rejected such a vision anyway. Since he'd never had a woman before, the sanctuary of the dark was immense; he would have killed anyone who violated it. Later, upon leaving the hotel, when she nearly gave in to curiosity and turned on the light after all, she never knew that she had survived only by virtue of having left the light off. In the total darkness he quickly became hard; his erection was a response to the invisibility of the moment, the blur of the frantically waning millennium nowhere to be seen. Within seconds he was already shuddering toward an orgasm. Sensing this she released him from her mouth, and took him in her hand as she knelt on the bed away from him; with trepidation he ran his hands forward along the downward slope of her back to her hair. She put him inside her. Blood roared to his head like a drug. Savagely he pulled her to him. When he heard her gasp and whimper into the pillow where her face was buried, he was at first confounded and then appalled by the lurking presence of love.

Nude Men

Amanda Filipacchi was born in Paris in 1967 and grew up in a bilingual household. When she was seventeen she moved to America to attend Hamilton College. After graduation from Hamilton she went on to receive a Master of Fine Arts from the Columbia Writers Program. Nude Men, her debut novel (widely praised for its intelligence, humor, and distinctly fresh, off-beat viewpoint), was translated into ten languages. Filipacchi explores contemporary sexual mores with imaginative verve and beguiling brio. Funny, energetic, and full of irresistibly odd touches, the book possesses a uniquely original perverse charm. She currently lives in Manhattan, and is at work on her second book, a surreal novel about an oceanographer and a kidnapping with a twist.

SHE GREETS ME AT THE DOOR, WEARING SOME SORT OF dressing gown or kimono. A goldish kimono.

In the middle of the room is set up the largest canvas I have ever seen her use. It is square, as tall as me. She says she will do a vertical, life-size portrait of me. She wants me to pose standing up.

I feel strange just standing there, stark naked, without even leaning against anything, without the slightest thread of satin to decorate me, to hide me, to pull one's attention away from my nakedness. Next to me, Henrietta has placed a stool, on which is a tray of canapés. There is also a glass of champagne and the inevitable marzipan, which today is in the shape of little pink elephants. She has an identical tray next to her easel.

She tells me I'm allowed to move my right arm and my jaw, to eat the food. I eat a pâté canapé, lick my fingers, and say, "I'm glad you feel like painting again," just to make conversation. "Are you now going to concentrate more on your serious art than on your commercial art?"

"Don't talk," she says. "Let's just appreciate the food and the sensual pleasure of creation."

So we pose and paint and eat in silence for a few minutes. Then she starts talking. Light, pleasant, amusing, unmemorable, insignificant conversation. I feel good, even though I've been standing virtually motionless now for about half an hour. I feel I could stand here many more hours, as long as there's a steady supply of canapés, champagne, marzipan elephants, and unmemorable conversation.

She gets up once in a while, to change my position slightly. One inch to the right, feet closer together, one step back— Wait! I don't want to get too far from my stool of marzipan elephants and insignificant conversation. We'll bring the stool closer, she says. Yes, closer, I sigh, comforted, as I bite off the trunk of a little pink elephant.

She goes back to her seat but soon puts down her paintbrush again. "Your position is still not quite right," she says, and adds pitifully, "Sara would have known right away what was wrong."

I am moved by the sadness and truth of that statement. I want to wrap my arms around Henrietta, I want us to cry into each other's necks, the poor mother. But I don't dare leave my carefully frozen position, for fear of displeasing her.

She gets up to fix my stance again. She walks behind me, and I wait with curiosity to see what adjustment she will think of this time. For a moment I hear nothing. Then I feel two warm, soft bumps of flesh against my back. I could swear there's no kimono cloth between my back and those fleshy bumps, but maybe I'm wrong, though I doubt it, but maybe I am, but no, but maybe.

Henrietta could not possibly be trying to seduce me. One does not stand behind someone, with one's breasts pressed against their back, when one is trying to seduce them. She must be doing something else.

"What are you doing?" I ask casually. My voice is not betraying my eyes, which are open wide in surprise.

"Changing your position," she answers.

That's what I thought she must be doing. I am reassured and relieved. But the next instant I feel her whole naked body against my back. Definitely no kimono cloth in between.

"You're changing my position?" I ask, just to make sure I'm not misinterpreting what I'm feeling.

"In a sense," I hear her say softly.

"Would you care to elaborate?"

She kisses the back of my neck and then my shoulders. Her

hands slink around my waist and move up toward my chest, not wanting to be too daring at first, I suppose. She slides her fingers through my hair, grabs a handful, pulls my head back and to the side, and kisses my lips. She can do that because she's tall.

"I meant verbally," I say, my voice sounding peculiar, because my head is cocked back so far and twisted so unnaturally. I am looking into her eyes at a strange angle.

"No words," she says, and kisses me again.

"I don't know if we should do this," I say, certain that I must look like a chicken with its neck broken.

"You have no choice," she says.

"Really?" And because of movies, I instinctively look down to see if she's holding a gun. I am puzzled that she's not.

"Then why do I have no choice?" I ask.

" 'Then'? Why do you say 'then'?"

"I mean 'then' as in, 'Since you're not pointing a gun at me, *then* why do I have no choice?' "

"That's not quite grammatical, I don't think."

"Neither is that."

"I know," she says.

"Well, mine made sense with my train of thought."

She kisses me.

Family Night

After a brief career as a poet, Maria Flook authored two novels, Family Night *and* Open Water, *and a collection of short stories,* You Have the Wrong Man. *This excerpt is taken from* Family Night, *which won a PEN American/Ernest Hemingway Foundation special citation. It's a joltingly powerful story of a quintessentially modern American journey replete with edginess and dark carnality. Flook teaches writing at Bennington College and lives in Truro, Massachusetts.*

MARGARET SMILED AT TINA'S ENTHUSIASM. SHE DIDN'T mind undressing before her sister. She wondered if Tracy would want to bathe. As soon as she was naked, Tina lifted a ladle of water and splashed it across her back. Margaret held her breath in the cold spray, but she turned in a circle as her sister dipped the ladle into the bucket and doused her with the icy water.

"You look beautiful," Tracy told her. "Like someone from another time."

"Like Venus," Tina said as she tipped the utensil over Margaret's shoulders.

"This must be how everyone bathed for centuries. These erotic water rituals," Tracy went on. He was trying to get something going.

Margaret lathered with the Castile soap. It felt hot, the peppermint burned the corner of her eye, it stung her as it washed down her legs and swirled through the small arrow of hair. It seemed to numb her. She said so, and Tina told them that in ancient medicine, mint was an anesthetic.

"I should have had some mint when I had my appendix out," Tracy said as he pulled his jeans off and moved behind Margaret.

"Oh God, he's going to try something," Margaret told Tina. She didn't like her sister seeing this.

Tina said, "Some people just invite rape. It's a *fait accompli.*"

Margaret looked at her. "You believe that? You're crazy."

Tina was working the pump handle until the bucket was refilled; then she went back to scooping the water and sifting it over them. "The Egyptians used mint in their embalming, mint and anise," her sister said. "Comfrey, fennel, costmary, lavender, coriander—" Tina stopped naming herbs when Tracy took Margaret's soapy wrist, pulling her hand to him.

"Shit, Tracy!" Margaret said.

"Give me a hippie hand-job," he whispered.

"Out of the question," she told him.

He was smiling. A smile in the dark looks strange, disembodied; you can't be sure what it means because the eyes aren't lighted. Tracy knelt down and scooped his hand over the bronze floor of mud then slapped the clay against her belly, smoothing it down. Margaret started to walk away, but he held on to her. She stood there. He pushed a handful of mud against her cunt, rubbing it into the slit. Margaret felt the velvety grains of earth, gritty but pleasing as he touched her, sculpting notches around her labia. The clay began to tighten over her belly and along the inside of her thighs. Tracy kept dabbing it on until she felt weighted, heavy with pulses. She dipped at the knees when it rocked over her and she saw her sister's teeth, luminous flashes. Tracy patted the mud against Margaret's thighs and over her buttocks, then he stood up. He fitted himself behind her, tugged her hand until she took him. His brief, omniscient shuddering was sudden and afterward he leaned into her. He rested his forehead against the shallow plane between her shoulder blades; she felt his eyelashes swipe her vertebrae.

Margaret pushed herself away from Tracy. The clay coated her legs and belly, glimmered with a metallic swirl and she thought of the starlet in *Goldfinger*. Wasn't that girl painted head to foot until she suffocated? Hollywood made it look glamorous. She grabbed the sponge from the bucket and she began washing the whorls of mud from her belly and thighs; her muscles rippled, her breasts bounced in tight shivers under her vigorous scrubbing. Her sun poisoning looked raw, pink as cigarette burns above her knees. She had to jerk the handle on the pump to wash herself better, and she straddled the stream, the clay rinsed white in the flow. Her cunt was stinging from the mud's abrasion or it was the icy water, knifing her until a new wave ascended, but she turned away from it. She threw the sponge down and picked up her clothes. "You go too far sometimes, Tracy," she told him.

"They charge a lot of money for this mud treatment in Vichy and those other spas," he said. He was telling Tina they might have a new angle if the Christmas trees were blighted. Margaret couldn't bring herself to walk away into the darkness and she waited for him as he washed himself. When he was finished, he grabbed her elbow and led her away from the muddy circle. Margaret could hear the pump screeching as her sister worked the handle, the water slicing a bevel in the mud.

"Processing"

Mary Gaitskill was born in 1954, grew up outside Detroit, and lives in New York. She wrote two short story collections, Bad Behavior *and* Because They Wanted To, *and a novel,* Two Girls, Fat and Thin. *Her writing is searingly honest and frank, and has been regarded as pathbreaking in bringing literary sensibility to lesbian—and, in fact, all manner of sexual—relationships. She is a visiting lecturer (1996) at the University of Houston. This excerpt, from the short story* "Processing," *appears in the collection* Because They Wanted To.

THE WEEK AFTER I MET FREDERICK, I WENT TO A PARTY celebrating the publication of a book of lesbian erotica. I was talking to two women, one of whom was facetiously describing her "gay boyfriend" as better than a lover or a "regular friend." She said he was handsome too, so much so that she constantly had to "defend his honor."

"You mean he's actually got honor?" said someone.

"One should always maintain a few shreds of honor," I remarked. "In order to give people something to violate."

"I don't know if that qualifies as honor."

"It's faux honor, and it's every bit as good for the purpose I just described."

"Can I get you a drink?" There was a woman standing off to the side, listening to me. I was startled to see that she was the woman who had taken a Polaroid of Frederick and me. Even in a state of apparent sobriety she emitted an odd, enchanting dazzle.

"Yes," I said. We took our drinks out onto the steps. A lone woman was sitting there already, smoking and dropping cigarette ash into an inverted seashell. When she saw us, she said hello and moved to the lowest step, giving us the top of her head and her back. Because she was there, we whispered, and our whispers made an aural tent only big enough for the two of us.

"I wondered if I'd see you again," she said. "I wondered what happened with you and that guy."

"Nothing," I said. "It was a one-night thing. We didn't even have sex."

"I also wondered if you like girls."

"I definitely like girls." I paused. "Why did you want to get me a drink just now?"

"What do you think? Because I like your faux honor."

"Because it has cheap brio and masochism?"

"Exactly!" I felt her come toward me in an eager burst, then pull away, as if in a fit of bashfulness. "But we shouldn't be so direct," she said. "We should maintain our mystery for at least two minutes."

I felt myself go toward her in a reflexive longing undercut by the exhaustion that often accompanies old reflexes. "I'm Susan," I said.

Her name was Erin. She was thirty-two years old. She was trying, with another woman, to establish a small press and, to this end, was living on a grant that was about to run out. She was reading a self-help book called *Care of the Soul* and *Dead Souls* by Gogol. She had been taking Zoloft for six months. She seemed to like it that I'd written a book of poetry, even if it had been ten years ago. She said that she sometimes described herself as a "butch bottom" but lately she was questioning how accurate that was. I told her I was sick of categories like butch bottom and femme top or vice versa. I said I was looking for something more genuine, although I didn't know yet what it was. She said she thought she probably was too.

"That picture you took of me was sad," I said. "I look sad in it."

I expected her to deny it, but she didn't say anything. She reached between my legs and, with one finger, drew tiny, concentrated circles through my slacks. It seemed a very natural thing. It seemed as if she thought anyone could've come along and done that, and it might as well be her. This wasn't true, but for the moment I liked the idea; it was a simple, easy idea. It made my genitals seem disconnected from me, yet at the same time the most central part of me. I parted my lips. I stared straight ahead. The silence was like a small bubble rising through water. She kissed the side of my lips, and I turned so that we kissed full on. She opened her mouth and I felt her in a rush of tension and need. I was surprised to feel such need in this woman; it was a dense, insensible neediness that rose through her in a gross howl, momentarily shouting out whatever else her body had to say. I opened in the pit of my stomach and let her discharge into me. The tension slacked off, and I could feel her sparkle again, now softer and more diffuse.

We separated, and I glanced at the woman on the steps, who was, I thought, looking a little despondent. "Let's go in," I said.

Inside, we were subdued and a bit shy. We walked around together, she sometimes leading me with the tips of her fingers on my wrist or arm. Being led in such a bare way made me feel mute, large and fleshy next to her lean, nervous form. I think it made us both feel the fragility of our bond, and although we spoke to other people, we said very little to each other, as though to talk might break it. We assumed she would walk me home; when we left, she offered me her arm, and I fleetingly compared her easy gallantry with Frederick's miserable imitation of politeness.

As we walked, she talked about people at the party, particularly their romantic problems. I listened to her, puzzling over the competence of her voice, the delicacy of her leading fingers, the brute need of her kiss. Her competence and delicacy were attractive, but it was the need that pulled me toward her. Not because I imagined satisfying it—I didn't think that was possible—but because I wanted to rub against it, to put my hand on it, to comfort it. Actually, I wasn't sure what I wanted with it.

We sat on my front steps and made out. "I'd like to invite you in," I said, "but it would be too much like that guy—I meet you at a party, bring you home." I shrugged.

She nodded solemnly, looked away, looked back and smiled. "So? I thought you said nothing happened anyway."

"He made out with me and I sucked his dick, and then he acted like he didn't want me."

"That's sort of harsh."

"Yeah. He acted like he was being nice, and I believed him, but then when I saw him again, he acted like a weird prick."

She embraced me sideways. "That sort of turns me on," she said. She nuzzled my neck, and the feminine delicacy of her lips and eyelashes was like a startling burst of gold vein in a broken piece of rock. I slid my hands under her shirt. She had small, muscular breasts and freakishly long nipples, and there was faint, sweet down all along her low back.

I invited her in. She entered the living room with a tense, mercurial swagger that pierced my heart. We sat on the couch. "So," she said. "Do I get to be the bad boy? Are you gonna suck my cock?"

"Don't," I said. "He hurt my feelings."

"Awww." She knelt between my legs, with her hands on my thighs. Her fingers were blunt and spatulate, with little gnawed nails. "If I say something wrong, it's because I'm not sure what to do. I'm not used to this. I want to please you, but you also make me want to . . . I don't even know."

"I'm not sure what I want, either," I said. "I think there might be something wrong with me."

She held my face in her hands. "Let me make it better," she said. She looked at me, and her expression seemed to fracture. Abruptly, she struck me across the face, backhanded me and then struck me with her palm again. She checked my reaction. "Open your mouth," she said. "Stick out your tongue." I did. She started to unzip her pants, then faltered. "Um," she said, "Susan? Is this cool?"

"Yeah."

When we were finished, I walked her out the door onto the porch. Using her ballpoint, we wrote our numbers on scraps of paper torn from a flyer that had been placed on my doormat to remind me to fight AIDS. She held my face and kissed my cheek and left.

⊰ REBECCA GOLDSTEIN ⊱

The Mind-Body Problem

*Rebecca Goldstein graduated from Barnard College in 1972
and received a Ph.D. from Princeton in 1976. After teaching
philosophy at Barnard and writing a treatise on the body
(from a philosophical perspective), she turned to fiction. Her
debut novel,* The Mind-Body Problem, *about what it's like
being married to a genius, is filled with humor and intelligence. Philosophy has probably never been as entertaining.*

"YES. TRIVIALITIES LIKE HUMAN FEELINGS." HE LOOKED AT
me for several seconds, considering me. "You know, Renee,"
he finally said, "you are an essentially trivial woman. You have
a lovely face and body, but in essence you are very trivial."

I felt as if I had flunked my final exam, my very final exam.

I had become quite frigid by this time. It was my first experience of sex without desire. What a cold, cold thing it is,
the bare, dry facts, scraped clean of the film of desire.

On one of my trips into New York at about this time, I
overheard a group of pubescent girls, maybe thirteen or fourteen years old, chattering and giggling, and I caught the phrase

"making out." It startled me. I hadn't heard the phrase in so many years. In fact, now that I heard it again I was surprised it still had a place in adolescent vocabulary. For the phrase is used by those who are teetering on the brink, approaching without yet plunging in to the inestimable depths; the plunge known in that same vocabulary, at least as it was employed in my adolescence, as "going all the way." I hadn't thought teenagers now hesitated on the other side long enough to have use for a phrase like "making out."

I sat there on that subway remembering the time of my own delicious teetering with Hillel, when each step closer convinced us of the overwhelming power and mystery of what lay beyond. And now I had passed through to that great knowledge, and this was the reality. It was horrible. (How many other mysteries would end this way, were one finally to see through them? How desirable *is* the parting of the mists?)

I was incapable of arousal with Noam. My flesh under his touch was dead, only stirred now and then by a ripple of revulsion. For a while I pretended orgasms, but then I saw that I needn't make the effort. Noam wasn't watching.

He was staring away, and not only in bed. When he wasn't raging, he was absent, at least in spirit. That day he first sat down next to me on the dinky, we had been strangers to one another; and yet he had held my eyes with such direct intensity that I was made uncomfortable by the implied intimacy. And now we were man and wife, and that vivid gaze, which had first settled on me with admiration as I stood in the surrounding circle at Loft's party, that gaze which had directed all its brilliance and enthusiasm at me in the course of the accompanying conversations, that gaze, and all its intensity, had turned away.

Frigidity we call it in women, impotence in men. The terms reflect, I think, the male point of view. But there's coldness and want of power on both sides. I certainly felt impotent, a thing of naught.

I briefly considered masturbation, as (and in much the same spirit) I considered jogging: as something that, no matter how unpleasant, might be good for me. For I thought it possible that my body would go quite dead, become incapable of ever feeling pleasure again; and that, at least according to the collective opinion of the day, couldn't be healthy. But then again perhaps a sexual death, if possible, would be the most reasonable solution. I had once read a former inmate's account of prison life, and he had written that after several months of celibacy all desire had mercifully vanished. Prison had been much easier after that.

But could it all be made to disappear? Despite my respect for Noam's views, and Noam's contempt for Freud's, I couldn't rid my thinking of such concepts as repression. I had an image of molten libidinous matter, seething in the psychical depths, which could be buried but never destroyed. And eventually the volcanic eruptions in personality would come, the lava of the libido spewing forth in geyser-like behavioral aberrations. The best one could hope for would be sublimation (which might, if Freud was right, even make a genius of me). Is it possible to die a merciful sexual death? And where would that leave one?

Sartre says the object of sexual desire is a "double reciprocal incarnation," most typically expressed by the caress: "I make myself flesh in order to impel the Other to realize *for herself and for me* her own flesh. My caress causes my flesh to be born for me insofar as it is for the Other *flesh causing her to be born as flesh.*"

But it seems to me that even deeper than Sartre's object lies another: a double reciprocal mattering, the most typical expression of which is the gaze. In gazing with desire on the Other I reveal how he, in my desire, takes me over, permeates my sense of self; and in his gaze I see how I similarly matter to him, who himself matters at that moment so much. It's *this* double reciprocal process that accounts, I think, for the *psychological* intensity of sexual experience. It answers to one of our deepest needs, a fundamental fact of human existence: the will to matter.

Noam had sadly missed the point in thinking the object of sexuality is no more, and no more interesting, than a sensation. His is the solipsistic view of sex, and it leaves out the complexity, the depth, and the reason this part of life matters so much to us. Without the Other and his gaze, the act is little more than clumsy masturbation. And so it was for me with Noam, who now was always turned away, psychically if not physically, like the man in the da Vinci sketch. Making love under such circumstances is hardly the powerful affirmation of mutual mattering it's meant to be.

To matter. Not to be as naught. Is there any will deeper than that? It's not just unqualified will, as Schopenhauer would have it, that makes us what we are; nor is it the will to power, Nietzsche, but something deeper, of which the will to power is a manifestation. (And who am I, daughter of a *shtickele chazzen* from Galicia, to argue with the likes of Schopenhauer and Nietzsche?) We want power *because* we want to matter. Neither sex nor power lies at the level of fundamental facts. Beneath are the heaving thrusts of the will to matter. And the will to create? to procreate? These too are expressions of the fundamental will. Deeper even than the will to survive. We don't *want* to live when we become convinced that we don't, can't, will never matter. That is the state which most often precedes suicide—always, I think, when the cause of suicide lies within.

To matter, to mind. Curious to compare the verbs we have formed from the nouns. What we mind is in our power, but whether we matter may not be—and there's the tragedy. Spinoza tried to help us out of it: We can make ourselves matter because of what we mind. No, no, rather: We shouldn't mind that we don't matter. *It*—of which we're a part—matters. Dissolve the individual will to matter in the objective picture of the whole. It's rather a drastic solution, but then perhaps nothing less will do. And does one thereby dissolve the individual? Is this the solution to the problem of personal identity? Is this will our very essence, with which we are and without which we are not? Perhaps. In any case, it's very close to the realization of the self. We no sooner discover that we are, than we want that which we are to matter. In spite of Spinoza.

Can anyone truthfully say, I don't matter and I don't mind? Not I. Of all my many mind-body problems, the most personally and painfully felt has been this: Do I matter as a mind or do I matter as a body? This is the problem that produces the pattern, the pendulum swings of my dangling life. But some-how or other I *must* come out mattering.

And where was I now? I had hoped, like the good fairy tale taught, to save myself by marrying Noam. My mattering to him, who himself mattered so much, was going to do the trick. It had always been a battle against self-hate, and that's a bloody battle. I certainly didn't have the stuff to stand up to Noam's attacks, his palpable contempt. If I have quaked before every idiot's judgment, if the shrug of the shoulders has always been a movement I'm incapable of executing, imagine how it was to be standing before the Highest judge, the Genius, before whom no invalid inference could be hidden, and to hear the verdict delivered: You are damned, you are dumb.

The sex was the least of it, if that can be comprehended. I am concerned to distinguish my voice from that great chorus of sexual lamentation being sung by women throughout the land, in first novel (the autobiographical one, right?) after first novel. The voices are different. Some sing raucously, some delicately, some with a constant whine. But all are singing the Marital Blues:

My husband don't please me
Takes all but don't give me
In-out and he's done
And I never come.

I don't say that he beats me
But the way that he treats me

Makes me feel old and done
And I never come.

Then the Love Affair, and the music changes. . . to Rachman-
inoff, climax after climax.

Then he came
And I came. . . and I came. . . and I came. . .

Till back we go to the blues:

That bum went off humming
And there's no second coming.

Women being done wrong, with all the action below the
belt, pelvic drama. I'm not denying the pleasure and pain involved. (Who was it who said bad sex is better than no sex at
all? What a blessed sexual existence he must have enjoyed.)
Sex that's gone dry and tasteless, that one can swallow only
with effort, is one of the more unpalatable experiences life
offers. Especially when one is remembering or imagining the
cognac-soaked flambé possibilities. But orgasms—weak, few or
nonexistent—are not the stuff of tragedy.

The Other Side

Mary Gordon was born in Far Rockaway, New York, and was educated at Barnard College and Syracuse University. She is the author of four novels, Final Payments, The Company of Women, Men and Angels, *and* The Other Side, *a short story collection,* Temporary Shelter, *and a book of essays,* Good Boys and Dem Girls. *Most recently she wrote an autobiographical account of how she discovered the true nature of her father's background, which he had always kept hidden. All of her work has met with critical acclaim. She is one of America's best writers, unique in her deeply humane, eerily perceptive intelligence. This excerpt is from* The Other Side. *Mary Gordon teaches at Barnard College.*

BEFORE OR AFTER THEY MADE LOVE, HE COOKED FOR HER; she didn't like to be naked when he cooked and she didn't want to be clothed. He wore a robe, but she had nothing suitable. So she bought a thin pink cotton nightgown. It allowed her breasts and sex to be visible, but why not, she thought, why not with him? The neck was high and square. A lace border grazed her collarbone.

She walked into the kitchen wearing her new nightgown. He was cooking. She'd just bathed; the ends of her hair were damp; the lilac scent of her expensive soap was on her skin. It was hot in the apartment. They hadn't yet made love, but she knew how it would be that night: slow, expressive, punctuated by pauses filled with reverie, returns to languid, half-absent caresses, leading, almost surprisingly, to an active end. Sex that night would be in favor of the female, she thought, walking towards him; that night, she predicted, women all around New York would sleep in peace.

"How nice you look," he said. He put his spoon down. He forgot his cooking; he walked her to the bed; he asked her to keep her nightgown on when they made love.

Kissing the lace border of the nightgown, he followed it, half-inch by half-inch, with his lips.

"That nightgown brings back pleasant memories to me," he said afterwards. "We'd go away each summer to the country. To the mountains. There were these houses, farmhouses called *kuchelaines,* big houses, with several families. There were these long days when you did nothing. Rainy days when you played games with other children. Or fooled around on a piano. Or one year someone played the banjo. Another year some aunt had a guitar. It was just women and children, mothers, grandmothers, aunts; the fathers came on weekends, some of them, or on vacation for two weeks. In the evening, all the children would take baths, and then we'd go outside for the last moments of light. The dark would come, the mothers would turn the lights on, you could see them sitting in the kitchen, at the table, playing cards. They were happy to leave us alone. Everyone's hair was damp from their baths. Like yours," he said, kissing the ends of her hair. "The girls wore cotton nightgowns with lace trimming. Like yours," he said, kissing the lace border once again. "The cloth of those night-gowns was fresh and beautiful. It had a beautiful fresh smell. And the grass smelt wonderful. It wasn't sex, but all your senses were alive and at the same time calm. Well fed."

The Mambo Kings Play
Songs of Love

*Oscar Hijuelos was born in New York City in 1951 to Cuban
parents. In addition to the Pulitzer Prize–winning* The
Mambo Kings Play Songs of Love, *his novels include* Our
House in the Last World, The Fourteen Sisters of Emilio
Montez O'Brien, *and* Mr. Ives' Christmas. *Hijuelos is a mar-
velous storyteller in the time-honored Latin-American tradi-
tion, who writes of complex family relationships with warmth,
sensuality, nostalgia, and love.*

BECAUSE OF THE TOUR, CESAR SPENT HIS THIRTY-EIGHTH
birthday in Chicago. They were holed up in an old twelve-
story hotel called the Dover House, on the Northeast Side,
overlooking Lake Michigan, and he'd had a good day walking
along the shore with his brother and a few of the Mambo
Kings, clowning around, eating in nice restaurants, and, as
always, trying to kill time before the show. He certainly expected something more from the fellows than what he had
gotten. He considered himself their father, their Santa Claus,

their spiritual advisor, the butt of their jokes, and there he was, on his birthday, after a show, without any sign that his musicians would celebrate his birthday. So it was not as if he was impervious to pain. On a normal night out, he would have suggested a party, but he resisted the idea of initiating his own birthday celebration. After his fellow musicians had gone their separate ways, and Cesar and Nestor headed for their rooms, Cesar was the solemn one for a change.

"Well, happy birthday, *hermano,*" Nestor said, with some embarrassment in his voice. "I guess I should have said something to the band."

And that little incident tapped into Ceasar's feeling that went back a long way to Cuba: that no one does a thing for you, so you must do it yourself.

Feeling downcast about turning thirty-eight, and about being alone on the night of his birthday, Cesar opened his hotel room door and clicked on the light; he slept in a bed that was up against a wall of mirrored tiles. Stretched in front of those mirrored tiles was a beautiful long-legged woman, head of thick black hair propped up on an elbow, body luscious and naked.

Taking in the spectacular curvaceousness of a body whose front startled the Mambo King and whose shapely bottom, soft and rounded as a swan's neck, was reflected in the mirror, he said, *"Dios mío!"*

And the woman, a brunette with big brown eyes, said, *"Feliz cumpleaños,"* and smiled.

She would be another acquaintance of his, an exotic dancer, Dahlia Múñez, who was professionally known as the Argentine

Flame of Passion. He and a few of the Mambo Kings had watched her dancing in a club on the South Side. When his fellow musicians saw how Cesar could not take his eyes off her that night, they hired her as a present to him, and there they were: she opening her arms and her legs to him, and Cesar hurrying to strip off all his clothes, which he left in a pile on the floor. Every woman he'd ever bedded down, he would think years later in the Hotel Splendour, said something to distinguish her lovemaking. And for the Argentine Flame of Passion it was the way she enjoyed the act of fellatio, actually liked the spill of his milk inside her mouth—or so she pretended. (And her technique! She would make his spectacular member even more spectacularly huge. She'd take the root of his penis above his testicles, which resembled jowls and were the size of good California plums, squeezing so tightly that his thing turned purple with the rush of blood and then got even bigger and then she would just roll her tongue around it, take him inside her mouth, lick him all over, pull, prod, and poke his member until he came.) She had other virtues, which kept them busy until past seven in the morning; they slept happily until around ten-thirty, when the Mambo King and this Dahlia fucked one more time, showered together, got dressed, and showed up in the hotel dining room, where his musicians were gathered to wait for their bus. When he walked in, they broke into applause.

A. M. HOMES

"Chunky in Heat"

A. M. Homes teaches writing at Columbia University, and is the author of three novels, Jack, In a Country of Mothers, *and* The End of Alice, *and a short story collection,* The Safety of Objects. *Her work is quietly disturbing, daringly fierce, and often boldly witty. She is a passionate and provocative taker of intelligent risks. Not surprisingly, she has written a great deal on psychotherapy and the doctor-patient relationship. This selection is from her short story "Chunky in Heat."*

HER THIGHS SPREAD ACROSS THE VINYL ROPES OF THE LAWN chair. In the heat they seem to melt into the plastic, seeping out from under her shorts, slipping through the vinyl as though eventually she'll begin dripping fat onto the lawn.

"Chunky?" her mother calls through the sliding glass door. The voice is muffled and sounds like a drowning person talking under water. "I'm running errands, are you coming with me?"

Cheryl shakes her head. Her second chin rolls across her chest, gliding on a layer of sweat.

"Why not?"

Her mother seems to be gurgling behind the glass.

Cheryl doesn't answer.

"I'm leaving now," her mother says, and then waits at the glass for several minutes before walking away.

Cheryl lies on the chair in the center of the backyard, her right hand plucking individual blades of grass, her eyes not focused but aimed at a bald spot of lawn, a remnant from another afternoon when she had a similar problem.

They call her Chunky in part after the candy bar, which used to be her favorite. Her mother started it.

Cheryl was eating a bar and refused to give some to her little brother. "Too small to share," she said, popping it all into her mouth, ending the discussion.

He called her Fatty and poked her in the stomach; his finger sank deep into her flesh.

"Your sister is just chunky," her mother said.

"You bet she is," he said.

After that he called her Chunky and then everyone called her Chunky, and then as if being called Chunky actually made her fatter, she truly was Chunky—and she hated that candy bar and switched to Mr. Goodbar but didn't tell anybody.

Cheryl is fat, only she didn't know it until now. Before this she always thought of herself as a big girl, a growing girl, a girl who could do anything. Now, in the heat, in the sun, she lies immobile and swollen. She feels larger and larger as if her breath is actually inflating her. She tries not to breathe as much, as deeply. Her double chin presses down onto her chest, onto her windpipe, and she feels like she is suffocating. Cheryl tilts her head back, establishing an airway.

She tilts her head and thinks of models in *Vogue* who seem like they can tilt anything, like they aren't people but fully articulated dolls like her brother's G.I. Joe—G.I. Joke she calls him. She thinks of thin people on beaches, with a breeze slipping over them. She realizes that because they are thin, they are aerodynamic. She pictures herself on the sand and sees a blob exactly like a jellyfish.

Two incredibly large insects, with wing spans like small airplanes, buzz past Cheryl. They buzz back and forth within a foot of her head, and on their second pass-by they lock together belly to belly like Siamese twins. Their wings beat against each other with a faint clicking sound. They are mating; Cheryl knows that. She knows what they are doing, but she doesn't know how. She doesn't know what they are doing it with. She can't see anything. The insects' green eyes bulge out of the sockets, their front feelers claw at each other, and Cheryl feels sick. There are too many sensations, too many distractions. She is writhing in her lawn chair, shifting her limbs, her balance. The chair rocks and lifts into the air as if it might tip and dump Cheryl onto the grass. She grips the armrests, thinking that holding tight will make her safe.

"I'm gonna get you, I'm gonna get you." Cheryl hears the voice of her next-door neighbor. "Oooh, I'm gonna get you now." There is a high-pitched scream, a squeal of pleasure. Her next-door neighbor is chasing his daughter around in the backyard. She is six years old. "Bet you can't get me. Bet you can't," she mimics and taunts her father.

"Oooh, I'm gonna."

"Enough," the mother screams and then there is silence.

Cheryl looks around the yard and back at the house. Everything is still and shadowless as if stunned by the heat, the light, and the peak of the day. The house appears flat, as if it's been cut out from a magazine and glued back into another picture. Even with the fence around it and the ivy from the neighbors' yard growing over, wrapping around like guy wires, it is as if at any moment the house might take off and disappear into the wild blue yonder. There are no anchors, no signs of life, no swing set, pool, barbecue, nothing except Cheryl in the backyard.

She looks at the house, but focuses on the sensations of herself in the heat, of her clothing in the heat, against her body. Cheryl wears her clothing like the protective coating on a cold capsule. Clothing divides her body into reasonable sections, arms and legs that need to be kept apart from other arms and legs, safe from the possibility of skin touching skin and rubbing itself raw.

Outside, as she sweats, her clothing separates itself from her body and begins to slip slightly, working against her, moving independently. When she breathes in, her bra creeps up and sticks, like a rubber band around her ribs, biting her and then creeping up again, higher, when she exhales.

In a moment of extreme consciousness, she sits straight up, reaches her hand up the back of her shirt, and releases the bra, sending it snapping across her chest like a slingshot. She pulls it off under her shirt and drops it, lifeless, onto the grass.

In the hot air the surface of her skin becomes tacky and the tops of her thighs touch and stick together, gripping each other in a vaguely masturbatory manner. She moves her legs to separate them. This touching and pulling apart causes a soft lip-smacking sound. Her thighs rub together even in her thoughts.

There is the distant sound of a doorbell, a sound like the tone in a hearing test. When you hear the beep, raise your finger. She hears the doorbell and then a muffled voice. "Chunky, Chunky, are you here?"

She hears the boy who lives next door, the boy who is three years younger than her, the boy she plays games with that they tell no one about. She does it because he wants to and she wants to and she can't find anyone her own age to do it with and besides she feels better doing it with him because she's bigger than him, and he does what she tells him to. He doesn't care that she's fat because he's getting to and he doesn't know anyone else who is getting to, and he likes that she is older because even though he can't talk about it anywhere, it gives him a new kind of credibility even if it's only in his mind. She doesn't let him see her actually naked; that's one of her rules and part of what makes it all right. He just sees bits and pieces but it's never too much, never overwhelming. He doesn't try to kiss her and she likes that.

"Chunky, are you here?" His voice is higher than it should be. She doesn't like it when he talks. "Chunky, I think you're home."

She hears him calling but doesn't answer. It doesn't mean she doesn't want him, but she can't bring herself to speak. She lies on the lawn chair and thinks of him coming around the house, into the backyard and finding her. She thinks of him topless, his shoulders looking new and too big for the rest of him. She sees him unzipping his shorts and pulling them down, his erection jutting forward like an extra limb, a birth defect. She spreads her legs and he comes towards her. She has to spread her legs very wide in order to make a space between her thighs. He kneels on the grass and pushes in.

He grabs her breasts and squeezes them again and again like they are the black rubber bulbs on bicycle horns. He pushes into her hard and quick and she can feel it everywhere. He slams in and the newest part of her, the freshest fat, the softest flesh, jiggles. Her hips, thighs, and butt jiggle. Her breasts jiggle each time and she loves it; she loves the jiggling.

This is the thing about being fat that no one mentions. Everything feels good, every square inch has incredible sensations, as if skin when stretched becomes hypersensitive, as if by stretching the skin to cover the fat the nerves become exposed or sharpened: it is not just her flesh rubbing against itself but the very sensation of its existence, hanging from her body, apart from her body, swaying, jiggling, touching things.

"Chunky, are you in there? If you don't answer I'm leaving."

She imagines him not on top of her, but apart from her except in that one place and every time he goes in she slides up on the sweaty vinyl so that when they finish her head is hanging off the end and he can barely reach her.

She imagines him and as she imagines him she slips her hand into her shorts. She imagines him and she pulls her shorts down to her knees. She digs her heels into the bottom of the chair and pushes up, raising her butt up off the chair. Her flesh pulls up and off the chair like adhesive tape being removed and it hurts a little and she likes the sting and repeats the thrusting until her skin is raw and sweat coats the chair like butter and she doesn't stick anymore. She pulls her shirt up to her neck so her nipples can get the air.

When she finishes and realizes she is half-naked, her pants caught at her knees, her shirt at her throat, the sensation of being outside, in the middle of the day where someone might see her—and suddenly she feels like someone, at least one person, is seeing her with her clothes all pushed up and pulled down—is too much and she has to do it again, this time more slowly, this time for an audience. This time, she pulls all her clothing off. She does it lying on her back, imagining someone seeing her doing it. All she's thinking about is people watching and she's not fat or thin, she's sex, pure sex, and as they're watching her she thinks they're probably doing it too and she likes that.

She remembers when she was a little girl, maybe five, her mother walked into her room and Cheryl was on her bed with her pants pulled down and her butt poked up in the air. Even then she liked to get the air inside her, on her.

"What are you doing?" her mother asked.

Even then Cheryl didn't answer.

She remembers feeling something more than embarrassed but she can't think of the word. Cheryl is getting too old for this. She is so old that it is embarrassing.

Cheryl is naked on her lounge chair. Her mother comes home. Cheryl hears the car in the driveway on the other side of the house. She hears the fan running, the a/c still on, and then she hears the car turn off and the fan is still going. The car door opens and does not close, and suddenly everything is all wrong.

Her mother slides the screen door open and calls "Chunky" without looking at her daughter. "Chunky, Chunky, I'm calling you," her mother says, without noticing Cheryl white and naked, lying like a beached whale. "Chunky."

Cheryl is trapped in her head. She is aware of herself naked in the yard, naked in the day. She is aware of her name being called.

She imagines her mother will go back in the house and dial 911. She will dial 911 and report that her sixteen-year-old fat daughter is lying naked in the family backyard on a chair from Kmart and fails to respond when her name is called.

"Sweetie," her mother says, and Cheryl wonders how many calories are in the word *sweetie* and then she realizes that it's just a word and it's fat-free.

"I went to the grocery store, do you want to help me unpack?"

Her mother says, do you want to help me, and she means it. She is perfectly willing to do it alone, but she wants Cheryl to know that if she wants to, if she'd like to do something other than sit naked in the yard, she can come in and help, but she is under no obligation. It is simply an option.

Cheryl likes unpacking. She likes opening things and, before putting them away, tasting just a little bit.

She stands up, peeling herself off the lawn chair with a long sucking sound, and walks towards the house. As she walks, her legs slip past each other with the same whooshing sound that corduroy makes. Her breasts and belly and butt bounce as she walks; they bounce with different beats but all in some strange syncopation, like a strung-out rhythm section.

She steps over the threshold. The contrast between light outside and the darkness inside makes the dark somehow darker and causes temporary blindness. For the first minute all she can see is the front door, straight ahead across the living room. It is open. She can see out into the light. She thinks of walking through the house and out the other side. The darkness seems to take her over, to swallow her. She stands still. There are mirrors on both sides of the living room walls. She sees herself as a large mass of unbelievable whiteness. She sees her shape, the scope of herself and her size. She feels deformed.

In the air conditioning she can feel herself shrinking, somehow getting smaller all over. She looks away from the mirrors and focuses ahead on the open door. Her mother is just outside bringing in bags from the car. The boy from next door passes by on his skateboard and looks in the door. He sees her and calls out her name, "Chunky." Cheryl stands there, sees him see her, hears her name, and still stands there. Without realizing it she drops her hand to her crotch, covering herself. Her mother comes in carrying three bags, looks at her, and says, "Get dressed, dear."

◄{ PAULA HUSTON }►

Daughters of Song

Paula Huston, a Californian, has received a National Endowment of the Arts Creative Writing Fellowship. Her stories were chosen for "Best American Stories" in both 1993 and 1994. This selection is from her first novel, Daughters of Song, *which in its finest moments mirrors both the emotional depth and technical intricacy of the Beethoven and Mozart the characters are trying to master.*

DAVID AND SYLVIA HAVE MOVED, SOMEHOW, FROM THE SOFA to the bed he arranged on the floor. She lies on her back, her lips bruised, her face wet with kissing, the white robe still cinched around her waist but the top open now, loose, like her legs. Like all of her. She lies there loose and decadent and caught in wave after wave of exhilarating warmth as David's hands move inside the furry robe. She drinks him in—his soft clean hair, his hot skin, the petal of his ear against her mouth. And then, with a hard moan, he pulls at the bathrobe tie; it comes apart like yarn; the robe falls open; cool air plays along her belly. She lies there panting, horrified and delighted, knowing he can see all of her, not caring.

He pulls away, standing up, and she starts to cry out, No!, then sees that he is undressing in the dim light and so she holds perfectly still, her arm across her forehead, watching him. His body is beautiful and compact, the body of a muscular young boy. How many times has he undressed this way for a woman? She follows every move greedily, taking him in: the way the hips are knit to the pelvis, the way the knees protrude, the smooth bands of muscle across the back, the deep dimples in the buttocks. She has never seen a penis before; now she will; she studies him in the half light—he is crouching to take off his pants, but he sees her watching him and turns toward her, straightening—and she thinks, How heavy it is! What a secret thing, in its dark nest of tangled hair.

"You've never done this before," he says, standing above her. It is not a question.

She shakes her head, mute.

He squats—she hears his knees cracking—and then slides under the sheet beside her. They lie for a moment, inches apart; they are both breathing hard and she can smell it again—the urgent energy between them. Now that the decision has been made—now that they know what they will do—everything has gone into slow motion; they have, in spite of the surging energy, all the time in the world.

He turns on his hip, propping himself up with one arm, looking down at her. His face is sweet with anticipation, the crushed look gone—he is perfectly happy at this moment, she thinks. I am making him happy, a man I don't even know.

With the other hand, he slowly reaches out and begins to stroke her — shoulder, arm, breast, belly, over and over, the gentlest brushing of his fingers against her skin. She smiles up at him, but she is trembling again. I am naked in bed with a man, she thinks. And I'm glad it is him, someone who knows what to do.

She swallows, and reaches out with her foot until she has found his. His toes are warm and blunt, his foot bony. She strokes it with the bottom of hers and he lets himself down — slowly, slowly — against the length of her until they are touching, feet to collarbone. His skin is dry, almost hot; she can feel the beating of his blood. For a moment she succumbs to terror — what am I doing? how did this happen? — and then she is melting into his flesh.

His soft hair in her face; the scent of soap and cleanliness. His lips along her jawline, traveling like silent blind creatures over her throat, her neck. He breathes into her ear and she feels the tip of his tongue, his teeth against her earlobe. He is moving against her gently — in no hurry at all, but absolutely focused on every cell in her body — and she is moving with him. She has never felt anything so beautiful, so pure, and she is astounded; she never thought it would be this way. She feels herself rising out of her body onto some plane where everything is warm and thick and rich with blood. For a moment her father's face looms before her — Sylvia! he is imploring, What are you doing? — but she thinks, How can this be wrong? This is so *beautiful,* so full of love — and we're both such good people. When David breathes, she thinks she can hear words;

she tries to hear what he is saying, and then she realizes he is saying her name, Sylvia, Sylvia, Sylvia, over and over.

She feels like crying again—everything is so warm, so kind—but she is aching too, yearning for something more, though she can't tell for sure what it is. Blindly, yearning, she moves her hands from his back, down, down, to the round, strong humps of his buttocks. She is whispering too—Please, she is saying—and he nuzzles his face into her neck and pushes her legs apart with his knee.

So *this* is how it is, she thinks. Like music. And then David is suspended above her—she opens her eyes and sees him, dark against the dim light—and he is holding himself with one hand, stroking her, up and down, back and forth, in the warm place between her legs; something tells her to rise up to meet him, and she does, arching her back.

His penis, warm and blunt, noses itself inside of her, and she almost laughs in triumph; suddenly, however, there is terrible pain and she cries out, but David doesn't hear her. He is moaning himself—is he in pain, too? Hot, hot pain; she feels seared inside. She turns her head on the pillow back and forth, back and forth, biting her lips. He rocks above her, pushing himself deeper and deeper, a desperate exploration. What is he hunting for? She is almost crying, he is hurting her so badly. What is he doing? And why has she let him inside of her? His face is contorted, he pants, he is like Bellyman in the final agony. Oh God, she moans. What is happening? Are we dying?

He is clasping her, he is pulling her closer and closer. She pants with pain, she is trying not to sob. And then, suddenly, he is calling, he is calling after something disappearing on the horizon; he calls out desperately; she can hear the utter loneliness in his voice. She moves her hands on his back, holding him there. No more dying, no more dying, she thinks. I won't let you.

He is lying on her body like something newborn. His skin is wet, his hair is wet, his breath sings between his teeth in the space beside her ear. She is throbbing deep inside; her flesh is torn; she wonders if she is bleeding. She is quiet, holding him, thinking: What does this mean? She cannot move her legs; the weight of him has pinned her to the floor. They lie this way for a long time and finally the pain subsides and becomes something else — something wet and aching and beautiful.

He stirs. His voice is distant, half asleep. "Did I hurt you?" he asks.

She is quiet. What will she answer? That it was the greatest of pleasures? That it was the worst of all pains? "A little," she says. "I'm okay." A small lie, for his own good. She is still dragging her soul back into her body. She is still searching for a missing person.

"May I stay?" he murmurs into her ear. "It's close to morning anyway."

If Jan comes by to take her to breakfast. If Francine calls looking for him. If anyone sees them leaving the brownstone.

"Well," she says.

He stirs against her. Her skin flutters. "If it's a problem, I'll go," he says into her hair.

She ponders this. If he goes, she thinks, she will wake alone;

she will rise in the morning and rub her eyes; she will wake from this fantastic dream. She will be Sylvia. If he stays, however. . . . Who will she be then, if he stays? At least she will have chosen this. At least it will be real.

"All right," she says.

The Blindfold

The Blindfold, *Siri Hustvedt's first novel, is a vividly com-*
pelling and fiercely intense tale of modern urban eroticism.
Full of intelligent and often startling risk-taking, the novel
possesses a uniquely jarring strangeness as well as a haunting
eloquence. She is married to the author Paul Auster (so, nat-
urally, she lives in Brooklyn).

MICHAEL PICKED ME UP OFF MY FEET AND CARRIED ME UP
the steps. His strength seemed remarkable, and I gave way to
it, letting my cheek rest against him. The last person who
carried me like this, I thought, was my father when he lifted
me out of the car where I had been sleeping. It was years and
years ago. Michael dropped me to my feet and took my bag.
I heard the jingle of keys, the sound of the door. He pulled
me inside. The light in the hallway shone through the cloth
over my eyes. Again he carried me. "You'll hurt yourself, Michael," I said.

But he didn't answer. He breathed heavily up the single
small flight of stairs, again let me stand while he opened the

door and drew me inside. I heard the door slam. I think he kicked it with his foot. Again I went for the scarf and again he stopped me, saying, "No, not now. I want you blind, just this once."

He kissed me, and it was good not to see him. He could have been any man. The anonymity was his and mine. Like a child, I felt that my blindness made me disappear, or at least made the boundaries of my body unstable. One of us gasped. I didn't know who it was, and this confusion made my heart pound.

We were in the other room. He had his hands on my shoulders and pressed me down on the bed. There was no light. He was fast, tugging at my clothes. Blind, I thought, the word stirring me. I'm going under. He had taken my wrists and held them above me in a gesture of conquest, and the recognition aroused me. I took the role and played it. The pleasure was in the staging, the idea of ourselves as a repetition of others. I knew this without saying it, felt my femininity as the game of all women, a mysterious identification in which I lost myself. He was caught too, and I wondered what he saw, whom he saw. It didn't matter. Let's drown, I thought, and I felt my pulse in my temples beneath the tight cloth. But then he seemed to race past me, to be overtaken by urgency. I moved my face close to his to kiss him, but he turned away. I searched for a new rhythm, but there was none. The blanket underneath me irritated the skin of my back. I wanted to tug at the blindfold, to adjust it, but he held my arms, intent, feverish. His skin was hot and clammy. I wandered from the drama in my mind, and my body went dead. His hands hurt my wrists, and

I struggled to free them, but he jerked me back onto the warm sheet and his fury shocked me. It's strange that one thinks at such moments, that thoughts move freely, that I remembered our conversations. Unspeakable acts, seizures of cruelty, Klaus. I choked on my fear, heard a noise come from me, an animal sound of alarm, and then I said, "No!" He put his hand over my mouth. "Shhhh! Someone will hear you." "No!" I cried out again, fighting him with my free hand. He grabbed it, but I kicked underneath him and screamed again. "Witch," he growled, and the name made me cry. He slapped me across the mouth. The pain astonished me. He doesn't know, I thought, he's still inside it. He can't know. Again he held his hand over my mouth as he pushed on me, dragging me to the end, but I beat his back with the fist of one hand and felt with my mouth for his fingers. I bit him, listening to the noise of his howl, and the sound made me happy. He pulled away, and I sat up, ripping the scarf from my face and throwing it down on the bed. I tugged at the blanket and draped it over my shoulders to cover myself completely. Moving away from him, I withdrew into a corner of my bed near the window and stared outside, gazing through the diamond bars of the safety gate into the airshaft below lit by the moon and distant neon. On the ground I saw some wayward garbage and stones. Where did the stones come from? I thought.

Michael grunted, and I turned my head to look at him. He sat at the edge of the bed, his bare legs apart, his shirt open. He was crying. I watched him, fascinated by his shuddering back and the unfamiliar sounds that came from him—short, uneven blasts of noise. He was ugly in his misery and it repulsed me. It's difficult to say how long we remained like that, how long it took before I felt the turn in myself. It came as a sharp, wrenching sensation in my gut, and then I pitied him.

He was speaking, the words disguised by sobs. What's he saying? I thought. I can't make it out. I inched toward him, taking the blanket with me, and then when I was very close to him, I put out my hand and hesitated. Finally I let my fingers rest lightly on his shoulder. The wet stripes on his cheek struck me as incredible. Fragments of sentences entered my head and then vanished. I opened my mouth, closed it. Then I whispered, "Why?"

He shook his head, folded his hands in his lap and rubbed the palms together. I stared at the fingers and saw the tiny wound where I had drawn blood on one knuckle. I shifted my gaze from his hand to the bed where the scarf lay still tied on the white sheet. Strange, I thought. Everything is strange.

Middle Passage

*In addition to his critically acclaimed novels and short stories,
Charles Johnson has published essays, book reviews, two collections of drawings and has written for various educational
television series. He is a richly imaginative, daringly complex
writer whose work consistently manages the difficult feat of
being at once thrilling and tender, fatalistic and funny. This
is from* Middle Passage, *which won the 1990 National Book
Award. Charles Johnson is the Pollack Professor of English
at the University of Washington in Seattle.*

"ARE THOSE FLOWERS FOR ME?" SHE ASKED. AGAIN, SHE
flashed that foolish, fetching, teasingly erotic smile. "Bring
them here."

I sat down beside her, kissed the cheek she turned up toward
me, then sat twiddling my thumbs. Meanwhile, Isadora took
a whiff of the flowers strong enough to suck a few petals into
her nose. She let the bouquet fall to the floor and turned to
me after moistening her lips with the tip of her tongue. Placing
her left hand on my shoulder to hold me still, she used her

right to grip the top of my slops, and pulled. Buttons popped off my breeches like buckshot, pinging against the bulkhead.

"Isadora," I asked in a pinched voice, "are you sure you want to do this? We can sit and read Scripture or poetry together, if you wish."

She made answer by rising to her bare feet, shoving me back onto the bed, and tugging off my boots and breeches. By heaven, I thought, still water runs *deep*. Who'd have dreamed these depths of passion were in a prim Boston schoolteacher? She was so sexually bold I began to squirm. I mean, *I* was the sailor, wasn't I? Abruptly, my own ache for detumescence, for a little Late Night All Right, took hold of me, beginning at about my fourth rib and flying downward. Soon we both had our hands inside each other's clothes. How long it had been since someone held me, touched me with something other than a boot heel or the back of their hand! And she, so much slimmer—pulling the gown over her head—was to me a figure of such faint inducing grace any Odysseus would have swallowed the ocean whole, if need be, to swim to her side. I kissed the swale by her collarbone and trailed my lips along her neck. Then, afraid of what I might do next, I slid my fingers under my thighs and sat on my hands.

Isadora twirled slowly on her toes, letting me see all of her. Now that she had my undivided attention, she asked, "Well, what do you think?"

"I'm not thinking."

"Good."

"But the animals. Can't you send them outside?"

"Rutherford!"

"At least cover up the birdcage."

"Don't worry, he's blind." Her voice was husky. "Just lie still."

Knowing nothing else to do, I obeyed. Isadora climbed over my outstretched legs, lowered herself to my waist, and began pushing her hips back and forth, whispering, "No, don't move." I wondered: Where did she learn this? Against her wishes, I did move, easing her onto her side, then placed my hand where it wanted to go. We groped awkwardly for a while, but something was wrong. Things were not progressing as smoothly as they were supposed to. ("Your elbow's in my eyeball," said I; "Sorry," said she; "Hold on, I think I've got a charley horse.") I was out of practice. Rusty. My body's range of motion was restricted by the bruises I had taken at sea, yet my will refused to let go. I peeled off my blouse, determined to lay the ax to the root like a workman spitting on his palms before settling down to the business at hand; but, hang it, my memories of the Middle Passage kept coming back, reducing the velocity of my desire, its violence, and in place of my longing for feverish love-making left only a vast stillness that felt remarkably full, a feeling that, just now, I wanted our futures blended, not our limbs, our histories perfectly twined for all time, not our flesh. Desire was too much of a wound, a rip of insufficiency and incompleteness that kept us, despite our proximity, constantly apart, like metals with an identical charge.

I stopped, and stared quite helplessly at Isadora, who said, "I thought this was what you wanted?"

"Isadora, I . . . don't think so."

She studied my face, saying nothing, and in this wordless exchange felt the difference in me. It coincided, I sensed by slow degrees, with one in herself, for in her disheveled blankets we realized this Georgia fatwood furnace we were stoking was not the release either of us needed. Rather, what she and I wanted most after so many adventures was the incandescence, very chaste, of an embrace that would outlast the Atlantic's bone-chilling cold. Accordingly, she lowered her head to my shoulder, as a sister might. Her warm fingers, busy as moths a moment before, were quiet on my chest. Mine, on her hair as the events of the last half year overtook us. Isadora drifted toward rest, nestled snugly beside me, where she would remain all night while we, forgetful of ourselves, gently crossed the Flood, and countless seas of suffering.

Dancer with Bruised Knees

Philosophy professor and fiction writer Lynne McFall has au-
thored two novels, The One True Story of the World *and*
Dancer with Bruised Knees. *Like her heroines, her writing*
is smart, tough, funny, and honest. It's also totally unsenti-
mental and intensely sensual. This short passage is from Dancer with Bruised Knees.

"REMEMBER THAT TIME IN PORTLAND?" HE SAID AS IF HE
were thinking the same thing. "Remember how we knocked
down the shower walls?"

"I remember. I had just stepped into the shower when you
walked in. You said, 'Sarah? Can I come in? I'm really dirty.
I don't think I can wait.'" I laughed and kissed him. "I said,
'Okay.'"

"I opened the glass door, and you watched me take off my
Levis and unbutton my shirt. I remember your wet hair clear
down your back." He unzipped my dress while he talked. "I
stepped in. I said, 'Do you need a little help with that soap?

The places you can't reach?' And you handed me the soap."
He helped me take off my black dress, and then I undressed
him, first the shirt unbuttoned slowly from the bottom.

"First you moved it over my breasts, in a circular motion,
like this, then around to my back, starting at my shoulders and
moving down. Then you kneeled and soaped my legs, beginning at my feet, picking up one foot, then the other, taking
your time, and when you did the bottoms of my feet I remember it tickled, and then you moved on to my ears, coming up
slowly, inch by inch."

"Like this?" he said.

"Yes. Like that." He kneeled at my feet. "By the time you
got to the tops of my thighs I couldn't wait."

He pulled me up from the couch and lifted me, remembering what came next.

"You picked me up and I wrapped my legs around your
waist, but the soap made me slippery and just when the
rhythm was good, when everything was right, I'd slip from your
hands."

He laughed. "I remember."

"You picked me up again, and again I slipped, down to the
bottom of the shower, the water running in my face."

"This time I've got you," he said, backing me up against the
wall.

"The next time you picked me up, you backed me into a
corner of the shower, and began again, taking it slow, and with
you inside me and the warm water running in my mouth, it
felt like the first time we made love, remember, how my heart
was beating so hard you could hear it, and I couldn't breathe?"

"I remember." He was kissing me and trying to talk at the same time. "When I heard the first tile give I didn't know what it was," he said, moving against me. "Then the second one fell, and then a whole row dropped onto the floor of the shower, just missing my feet."

"I remember we both laughed, but we didn't stop making love, and by the time we were through, the water was cold and the shower was destroyed, two whole walls caved in, the wallboard wet, in pieces, tile all over the shower floor."

"Here," he said. "That's it."

"The best part is what you said when we got the bill for over four hundred dollars."

"What? I don't—"

"We were sitting at the kitchen table, remember? You opened the envelope and flinched. I said, 'What's the damage?' And you ripped it in half and said, 'It was worth it.'"

He said, "It is."

Going to the Sun

James McManus has written Ghost Waves, Chin Music, Out of the Blue, *and* Going to the Sun *and a collection of poetry,* Great America. *He teaches at the School of the Art Institute of Chicago. His work is characterized by a vibrant energy, erotic edginess, and poignant lyricism. This is from his most recent novel,* Going to the Sun, *which is a compelling, urgent, and ultimately liberating book. McManus is the winner of the Carl Sandburg Literary Arts Award for fiction.*

STILL STANDING UP, IN THE LIGHT FROM A CNN BUSINESS report, we begin to undress one another. I can't reach high enough to pull off his shirt, so Ndele takes care of it for me. I hold up my arms while he pulls off my T-shirt. He drops it. We look at each other. He yanks down his little white underpants, dances sideways a little, steps out of them. Jesus. I take off my own jeans and panties, exposing my ridiculous tan, my proportions . . . Ndele's proportions are startling.

We kiss standing still. His cock bounces against my ribs, and I shiver. I touch it. It's heavy and warm and enormous.

When my legs start to tremble and buckle, Ndele holds me up by my nipples. I'm mortified by all of my cooing, my shudders, my awful and general noisiness. Oh . . .

I run my forearms back and forth across his wide chest. I've never seen anything like it: brutally sinewy, no hair except for a few glossy curlicues between two slabs of muscle. I rub both my hands up and down, digging in, trying not to scratch him too much. I can't help it.

He puts me facedown on the bed, holds me like that while he nuzzles my buttocks and squeezes the backs of my thighs. His yellow bedspread smells like cigarettes, sweat. I don't care. And now things are happening fast. I don't think I'm scared, but I'd rather be facing him. Much. To be able to see what he's doing, to watch it all happen. To touch him. I want things to happen more slowly.

He's licking the backs of my knees, running his teeth up and down while squeezing my ass with his hands; he's crushing the muscles together, lifting me up off the bed, short whiskers burning my skin. I want to turn over, but I like how he's holding me down. What should I do with my hands?

Things bounce and clatter as he kneels behind me. A beer can. A bedspring. A belt. Where's the gun?

Bracing myself against the wall, with Ndele behind me, I picture my room through the wall: my maps, my wet clothes, my bike leaning forward . . .

When I tell him I want to turn over, he pauses, then lets me. I grab him by his wrist and his leg and guide him down onto his back, on the floor.

"Lemme just slide on a jimmy."

I gingerly ease myself onto him. It hurts and it hurts and it doesn't.

"Lemme just get a jimmy!"

As I lower and turn myself onto him, down, can't go down, I'm shivering, can't catch my breath, but whoa baby. Oh Jesus! I can't close my eyes. I can't stop.

"Jesus, girl! Penny! You sure?"

He rolls on his side and maneuvers me onto the floor on my back. Gets on top. Holds my arms over my head. He slides his wet teeth across my hipbone and ribs and my pits. Bites my nipples—too hard and then even harder, but not too hard, either. Then harder. I need for these things to keep happening, to not ever stop, to never stop happening, Christ! . . .

He angles himself above me, forcing back my right leg with his chest. My kneecap is grazing my cheek—a position I've never been in. But it works. He lets my arms go while he guides himself in, oh good *God*, then grabs them again and yanks them back over my head. In the meantime he jams himself into me, hard. He already has this *momentum* that sears me and tears me—I really don't think I can take it or ever allow it to stop.

I picture the rest of our lives: a curly-haired daughter, gray stucco bungalow along the Pacific, dark bedroom furniture, an awkward parent-teacher conference in her second-grade classroom, at night, her rounded and excellent cursive on lined paper tacked to the long strip of cork above a minty green chalkboard. My kneecap is brushing my shoulder. I'm broken, torn open, can't budge. His rhythm has three little unholy hitches: it burns, jags, and jams me all up. My leg is beginning to cramp but I cannot, could never, resist him. Noises escape from the back of my throat I never approved of or planned and I'm telling him secrets and crying as he keeps banging into my bladder: over and over and over and over and over. My pussy convulses against him, all over him, over . . .

He releases my leg, changes angles, pushes my other leg all the way back, continues to fuck me like that. He holds me down hard on the floor and he fucks me. I'm helplessly licking my own bony shin, gasping and shivering, laughing almost, trying to tell him what good and how terribly good he is doing me, all this without using words. I do not have words. I don't have the strength or the words.

Later we lie perpendicular to one another, face-up on wrinkled linoleum, sweating and catching our breath. I'm having these sweet little spasms, then every few seconds a big one. I can't predict when they'll come next, or where. My upper lip and my eyelids are trembling. The side of Ndele's forehead presses against my left hip. His torso is twitching and heaving. He coughs. My right knee is up in the air, avoiding the wet spot beneath my right calf. A clump of warm shirt and some undies digs into my shoulder blade, so I shift my head sideways and use the bunched clothes as a pillow. The flutters won't stop in my cunt.

Ndele reaches up, grabs my hand. Just the fingers. His left hand, my left hand. Mmm. We lie here like this without talking. I can't make a fist, but my fingers slide over his thumb.

He says, "Hey."

Natural Tendencies

Joan Mellen was born in the Bronx area of New York, and educated at Hunter College and the City University of New York. One of America's most versatile writers, her twelve books include literary biographies Kay Boyle: Author of Herself and Hellman and Hammet: The Legendary Passion of Lillian Hellman and Dashill Hammet; true crime Privilege: The Enigma of Sacha Bruce; as well as that rarity—the perceptive and fair-minded sports biography—Bob Knight: His Own Man. She is perhaps best known for her groundbreaking film books, particularly The Waves at Genji's Door: Japan Through Its Cinema, Women and Their Sexuality in the New Film, and Big Bad Wolves: Masculinity in the American Film. She lives in Pennington, New Jersey, teaches creative writing and film at Temple University, and regularly writes "Arguments," essays on literary controversy for The Baltimore Sun. She is currently working on a memoir. This excerpt is from her vastly underrated 1981 novel, Natural Tendencies—her only work of fiction—about an American woman in Japan.

SEATED ON THE BED BESIDE HIM, SHE REACHED OUT TO make contact. But when she placed her hand on the back of his neck, he laughed for the first time that day, a loud, empty laugh. With one rapid movement that stopped just short of tearing it, he pulled open her blouse. She had never seen him like this. But it didn't occur to her to be afraid. There she was on his bed, Matsushita vigorously desiring her at last, and she tried to make herself feel joy, but she couldn't. She seemed not even to be ready for the anticipation of desire. But what more did she want? She thought, if only he had said something to me, told me he likes me. Then she brushed these doubts aside. What mattered was what he would do. He was going to show her what he felt.

When later she allowed herself to recall what he did to her that afternoon, she could only describe it as dreadful, a stage in her humiliation, the man at the airport exacting vengeance. But now, only slightly apprehensive, she welcomed whatever he wanted to do. It was Matsushita. She was with him in his apartment and they were about to be naked together again after all this long time.

Having opened her blouse, he made a quick motion. She was given to understand that she must remove the rest of her clothes herself while he watched, fully clothed. There was a hungry glint in his eye, and she could hardly bear to look at him. What she saw was the hunger of a *sated* animal whose appetite now exclusively, gratuitously, demanded blood for the sake of blood. When he began working his will on her, all she could think was she hadn't known that such a small man could be so strong. But suddenly now she wanted to be gone. Not yet knowing that he was about to inflict such sharp pain, she began really to fear the change in him. She had to force herself to suppress the misgivings that would have led her to the door, bidding him goodbye with a telling, "This is not what I had in mind at all." But she had stayed, willing herself to gladness at his new assertive mood. She had thought, At least it's not going to be like the last time, all that happy licking, lapping, and suckling which had caused her to lose all desire for him. Then he had been like a gentle old family pet greeting her after too long an absence.

And so, undressed, she lay back, willing that he come to her, yearning that he free her from herself, remove her to a place where the responsibility was his. He watched her, saying nothing, then, quickly, he threw off his clothes, exposing once more his satin skin, the well-muscled shoulders, arms, legs, thighs she had remembered, the heavy penis she had never seen—so surprisingly big for his size. Never taking his eyes, unclouded, piercing, from her face, he pinched her nipples so hard beneath his fingernails that involuntarily, not having time to remove the smile from her face, she reached to pull his hands away, to let him know that this hurt too much. It must have been the excitement of the moment. He hadn't meant to make her feel such pain; surely he didn't realize how much he was hurting her. But he wouldn't let go.

Finally he did, but only to bend over and bite down so fiercely on her right breast that a thin stream of bright red blood began to ooze out of her. Still he watched her face. Now angry she said, "Why did you do that?" And when he didn't answer, didn't even alter the gleaming, hostile expression on his face, she turned away, waiting for this part of it to pass. And still she didn't consider leaving. She thought, the last time, no matter how he tried, I wasn't aroused. He has decided it's violence alone that pleases me. And she did feel a rush of desire somewhere beyond her, not yet accessible but a tiny feeling, a promise. And so then she turned back to him and put her hand to his hair, those thick, sleek curls that moved right back into place, undisturbed by the movement of her hand. And when he then quickly moved down on her body, as if incited by that caress, inflicting quick, sharp bites, she put aside the pain of her sore breasts and even opened herself to him, wanting the feel of him, urging that he move still closer. And she allowed him to part her legs and enter her with his mouth, still unafraid.

When he found her clitoris, he bit down fast and hard, so hard she screamed out this time and thick tears flowed from her eyes. It hurt so much she couldn't move. In his face she saw the same calculation she had witnessed in his office when he was negotiating with Paul. Now he was negotiating with her. To what end? She stared at him as if ready now for the answer as to who he was. And in his eyes she read only the challenge, Have you had enough? Have you gotten what you want of me? Do you understand me now?

When she didn't say anything, didn't yield, just lay there the tears slower now, halted on her cheeks, when she still didn't call a truce that would admit that he wasn't going to give her what she wanted, he put his head down again inside her inert body and bit down once more, a wolfish, quick bite that was a sadistic afterthought. And this time after one shrill burst of pain it only ached.

And then she rallied too. She wasn't going to allow this to put an end to her chance with him. She would see it through. She reached out to him to let him know she was willing to endure whatever was necessary to have him. She touched his cheek, his ear, playfully, as if also to admonish him. He didn't have to hurt her that much. But she would let him know that she knew what he felt and so force him to acknowledge that the connection between them could withstand anything, even this.

He brushed her hand away. His face was now beet red, she thought, with arousal. And as if activated anew by her little gesture of affection, he threw her over and lifted her halfway to her knees. Even this she would tolerate, his taking her from behind. She was sore and she was numb. She didn't want it this way, had never been treated like this, but she had withheld herself from the real world, hadn't she. This must belong to the experience of men and women, this ascent through pain. And then she thought, why was Matsushita going so far? She tried to get away from him, gain time. She must somehow let him know that he had made his point. It was enough. Why any longer should they deny that tenderness awaited them, the sweet affection that had been there that first night in Yokohama?

"Not like this," she heard her voice, hoarse, thick, barely above a whisper. He neither said anything nor let go. She tried to squirm out of his grasp, but Matsushita, as slim as he was, seemed to have been possessed by the physical strength that madmen summon at their most demonic.

He already had one hand around her waist, two fingers of the other were digging inside her, fingernails scratching along, pain a prelude to more pain. No, he wasn't even going to use anything to make it easier, appalling as the prospect of Matsushita smearing her with grease might seem. This afternoon would be devoted exclusively to her assault, Matsushita whom she had thought so small that she couldn't feel him inside her, Matsushita forcing her to feel all the hard edges of his nature.

She didn't scream. She didn't even move. Instead she tried to pretend this was happening to someone else. As he ran his nails inside her, tracking, cutting little scratches, each sending a shrill shiver of pain through her, she submerged good sense, the wild physical struggle to save herself that alone might have made him stop. But she didn't want him even now to stop. He must do what he had to. He pulled his hand out and ground himself against her with power, with a size she hadn't thought could be his. A thick pushing back of flesh, unrelenting, tearing into muscle, leaving broken skin in its wake. One hand kept her up, the other now spitefully pinched her breasts for good measure as he rammed himself still farther up inside her. Still she tried to divorce herself from what was happening. This, she told herself, is what it's like to be the victim of an unnecessary surgical operation, flesh being torn apart as a punishment of fate, she getting what she was prepared to receive. Love, sex, desire, had become absurd. Could Matsushita be receiving any pleasure from this, she wondered? And she hated him for having branded her in blood with the anger of someone who so despised her.

All she could do was wait for his sick game to end. Then

this tenacious, leechlike thing, hardly a man, would let go and release her sore body back into her custody to heal as it would. But it seemed to take forever, Matsushita pounding his body against her as if even he couldn't relate this ordeal to sexual release because he hated her so much. Finally he drove faster and faster. Only in his finish did it resemble that first time. Five rapid thrusts and with a buried, strangled sound Matsushita could only have emitted in spite of himself it was over. He rolled off. She lay on her stomach, hurting too much to move sufficiently to cover herself. Matsushita got up and went into the bathroom without a word. There were streaks of blood, her blood, on the blanket. She felt ashamed, hated, used, discarded.

Katherine

Anchee Min was born in Shanghai in 1957. After coming to America in 1984, she worked at a variety of jobs, including waitress, messenger, model, house cleaner, fabric painter, and assistant at construction sites, while attending English as a Second Language classes. In 1990 she received a Masters of Fine Arts from the Art Institute of Chicago, where she studied filmmaking and music. Her shattering autobiography, Red Azalea, *about growing up in Mao's China became an international bestseller and is considered a small masterpiece. This excerpt is from her first novel,* Katherine. *Anchee Min lives and works in Los Angeles with her daughter, Lauryan Jiang.*

THE MOUNTAIN AIR BECAME FRESHER AND LIGHTER. I KEPT climbing. The sign said that I had arrived at the Shoulder of Beauty Tang, yet I saw no "shoulder." I couldn't figure out which part my feet were standing on—Beauty's neck, shoulder, or bosom? The near peaks looked like green dolphins shooting toward the sky from the ocean of mountains. I found a giant smooth stone under a pine tree. I lay down on the cool stone and felt peace. It was almost two. The sky was low — one moment it filled with thick clouds; the next, the sun broke through. There was no one else around. I breathed the air, dreaming about how Beauty Tang moved as she danced before her lover. At least she knew that the last thought the prince would have before he kissed death was of her. Wasn't that all the ancient concubine hoped for?

I closed my eyes. I could feel my thoughts calm down, slowly swimming between the veins of my brain. Time stopped. The Han Dynasty drum music faded from my head. I could hear my own sizzling thoughts crawling toward the shore of the brain's river. I heard a sudden laugh break through the quietness. It was familiar. I heard it again. I was not day-dreaming. I opened my eyes.

Across a deep valley, over on the opposite peak, about one hundred yards away, Lion Head and Katherine hung from a vine of ivy, lowering themselves toward a narrow rocky ledge. Lion Head was in control. He held Katherine on his lap, locking his arms around her waist. Bit by bit they swayed down.

I got up and hid myself behind a pine tree.

The valley was deep. They would fall if they were not careful. The mountain echoed with Katherine's laughter and screams.

I was surprised but not shocked. I knew there was an attraction between Katherine and Lion Head. I had admitted to her that I didn't love Lion Head and maybe I even encouraged her to seduce him. I didn't know why, but I always pictured the two of them together. I liked discussing Katherine with Lion Head. I once asked him to imagine how Katherine would moan when she made love. We both had fantasies about it. My desire to learn how Katherine made love to a man was stronger than my desire for Lion Head.

Was Lion Head different from other men? He was showing her risk, adventure, filling her ear with Chinese philosophy, Lion Head–style. A vinegar jar broke inside me, bitter and sour.

Lion Head was taking his time with Katherine. His body was glued to hers. I did know him well. He enjoyed the "sweet torture." He wanted her to feel his maleness, his determination, his heavy breath. I imagined her eyes closed, doing what he instructed. Was she trying to resist him? He would play with her by telling her to let go. He would tell her what ancient Chinese lovers did on ivy swings, rubbing and teasing their bodies. He would flood her with his storming knowledge of history. He would tell her that the process of rebirth was from moment to moment. He would explain the theory of impermanence of the world and tell her to resist the effort of trying to grasp things. He would suggest she listen to her body, and she would, and then he would make her his . . .

I felt admiration for Lion Head as much as jealousy. I remembered the way he seduced me. He did not have to touch me to get me excited. He was doing the same thing to this American woman. I was curious about her reaction to his touch, the touch of a Chinese man. My jealousy became insignificant for the moment. If this was betrayal, I deserved it because I was never sincere with Lion Head. I now realized how little I cared about him. My thoughts went to Katherine. I knew she couldn't love Lion Head. She told me more than once the image she had of Chinese men when she was growing up, how even the idea of being with a Chinese man seemed ridiculous. She told me that in America, Chinese men looked to her like "funny-looking little eunuchs." In a way, I wanted Lion Head to show her a Chinese man's muscle. I wanted to have him torture Katherine, mistreat her, beat the eunuch idea out of her head. I knew Lion Head would be good for the job, I knew he could make her beg.

I smelled the needles of the pine tree. Katherine once said that in America people feared passion, they laughed at those who loved too much. And still people longed to feel. What was she feeling now? Animal passion? Did the Chinese landscape make her bolder and stronger? I felt shivering and excitement.

They lowered themselves onto the small stone ledge. The space barely fit two. I saw Lion Head begin to unbutton Katherine's shirt.

Clouds began to obscure the sun, and the color of the mountain darkened. I felt a raindrop fall on my hot face. I rubbed my eyes, held my breath. Lion Head buried his face in Katherine's bosom. Gradually she stopped pushing him away. He started to explore her. Her invitation was silent. I could hear Lion Head groan. Katherine dared not move too much. If she did, they would fall into the valley.

He kissed her madly. He locked her fingers in his hands. His arms were strong. She seemed drunk with pleasure and frightened at the same time. She arched her chest, exposing her breasts. She raised one of her legs, slowly, and wrapped it around his hip as he devoured her.

She kissed him back, then stopped. She pushed him away. He insisted. He bit to open her shirt. She gave in. She began stroking his hair with her fingers. She was mothering him. Her swanlike neck bent back, her face toward the sky, and he entered her.

I could feel Lion Head move inside of me. I knew what Katherine was feeling. Her shiver of pleasure, her madness of wanting more. I entered Katherine through Lion Head. I could hear her moan, exactly as I had imagined.

He watched her, her swelling breasts, her milky skin and flaming eyes.

With the echo of Lion Head's groan, the mountain became enclosed in a white curtain of rain. The curtain grew thicker and finally blocked my sight.

The wildness disappeared from my mind's eye.

The Courtyard of Dreams

Anna Monardo's first novel, The Courtyard of Dreams, *is a perceptive and involving story of a first generation Italian-American woman struggling to come to terms with her old-world roots. It's an enchanting, evocative, and poignant love story.*

AS LUCA AND I GOT FARTHER AND FARTHER AWAY FROM each other in the daytime world, we fell more and more deeply into a nighttime world of no words, just touching. All night long we touched, in the dark, not looking. Deep into the night we made love, and often in the morning. Once I woke and found him standing beside the bed. His pants were unzipped, he was touching himself and looking at me.

"What?" I whispered to him.

"Nothing," he whispered back, but his eyes looked glazed. "Will you do something? Will you kneel down here on the floor by the bed?"

"Why?"

"I want to see you like that."

"Luca."

"Please."

It was all murmurs, my faint murmurs of protest, even as I slipped out of bed, his murmurs of encouragement and apology, frighteningly seductive, almost gasping, urgent, as he lifted my nightgown and tossed it across the room. I pulled a pillow in front of me and leaned against the side of the bed.

"Why this, Luca?" I said, but already I was excited. We both felt it: the bed wasn't big enough to contain us.

I couldn't see but I could almost feel the moonlight white across my back. Luca stood to the side of me, just looking, not touching, not saying a word. I didn't know what he was doing and this excited me even more. Then I heard clothes drop, his belt buckle clank the floor.

Three hot fingers moved lightly across my back, brushed the side of my breast. With one quick sweep, he lifted my hair up off my neck, then he was naked all along the back of me, kneeling behind me, his legs pressing tight inside my thighs. Trying to control himself, he pretended he was calming me. "It's OK, it's OK." His voice was so buttery and slow, but with shards of ice at the edges. "Relax," he said in Italian, then it was all dialect. "Just lean forward, into the pillow, that's right, like that, just lean." My knees were numb from the cold tile floor. Our small rug was crumpled under the bed. I tried to rest my feet on Luca's ankles to keep warm, but Luca kicked them away as he spread my legs wider.

I pulled him up inside me and he couldn't get deep enough. We sped each other on, rocking faster. We didn't lie to each other; there were no kisses, nothing like tenderness, and then even his voice stopped. Just breathing, gasping. We had crossed into some new place, close to violence, far from love. We were agreed. He wanted to turn me inside out, I wanted him to touch some spot buried deep, into the darkness and beyond it, into the light. I caught my face in the mirror across the room, saw the impatience in my eyes, my mouth, when, once, he slipped out of me. I heard the anger in his growl, and then saw the determined look in our eyes as both of us, desperately, led him back inside.

We were pushing so hard, the bed got away from us, and we were tired and I stretched out flat, my chest, my thighs, my stomach chilled against the tile floor. Then my back on the floor, then his back, over and over.

Afterward, we lay in bed silent and awake for a long time. By then we had stopped asking each other, What are you thinking? Our silences were cold and private and within them, we were each alone. I was wondering how many times Luca and I had made love during the past year. Innumerable. Soon I would be a woman who didn't make love with Luca. Who would I be? Would I change quickly? Or would I relinquish slowly like an immigrant, with small releases of the fist?

"Luca?"

"*Sì?*"

"*Niente.*"

"The Ring of Brightest Angels Around Heaven"

Rick Moody has written three novels, Garden State, The Ice Storm, *and* Purple America. *His writing is fiercely imaginative, darkly comic, and passionately cerebral. He lives in Brooklyn, New York. (And somehow, the previous two sentences are connected in some way.) This selection is from the title story of his acclaimed collection,* The Ring of Brightest Angels Around Heaven.

THEY SLEPT TOGETHER FIRST. THEY SLEPT TOGETHER BE-fore talking, and it was really, really sexy, the way he saw it. It was like the first time. He took off her skirt slowly. He liked to see how slowly it was possible to make love. He kissed her so slowly you didn't even know his lips were moving. How slowly? His movements were in increments smaller than mil-limeters. *The band with no name* was playing on the old, beat-up tape player, and the video camera was standing on a tripod, pointing out the window, and he was proceeding across her lips as slowly as possible. It could take hours before he would creep down along her neck, after pausing to dig an incisor into her earlobe, after pausing to suck on her tongue. Hours before he was aimlessly encircling her breasts with his fingertips. And then further down. He liked every second of it. He even liked unlacing her Doc Martens. Nakedness was never so naked. And then he touched her stomach. Women had gotten pregnant because of his irresponsibility before, once in boarding school, once after a weekend by the shore in Mobile, but he had been young then. This was his first time as an adult. The fact of it, the fact of fertility, was enormous and perfect like the shape of a particularly dangerous storm.

Her belly was small and trim. She didn't eat too well. *Just eat to avoid fainting,* she said. *Nothing more.* He traced his finger across her stomach as if he were painting cave paintings there, as if trying to render the moment of conception in some pictorial writing. As if trying to capture all the lives bound together in this notion of conception. What was so sexy about all this? What was hot about coming to the end of the profligate and wandering part of your life? What was sexy about suddenly wanting to accept responsibility? Maybe in part what was sexy was all the bad news, all the risk, all the difficulties. Maybe he wasn't thinking clearly about it at all. But maybe he was. Love was something that had the threat of bad news with it. Love was risk and obligation and caffeine addiction. Love was like watching the Tompkins Square riots on television. It was like hearing a guitar amp explode. It was like shooting coke for the first time. It was like watching the demolition of a tenement building and it was like remembering these pleasures years after they are gone.

And that was when she introduced the device.

—Hey, look, I have this thing I have to show you . . .

She reached over beside the bed where an ominous looking electrical kit was waiting.

—What the fuck is that?

The shame of being found out, of being located and then conscripted into the league of kinks, of being a guy who liked devices *and* wanted a family, this shame overcame him first. His resistance was first. He knew, in some atavistic part of his unconscious reserved for the pursuit of bodily woes disguised as pleasures, he knew what it was. He didn't know how it was going to work, but he recognized the control knobs on the box. They resembled the knobs that had driven the electric trains of neighbors in his boyhood. One of the dials was marked "course" and the other "adjustment."

This is an electrical stimulation box, she said. It's for the film. See? I'm getting interested in this idea that I can have like some sex club stuff in it. I could have, you know, couples using these marital aids. Like this one or Electra or something. From Orgone Romance Systems of Las Vegas. These ones here are the *instant kill switches* and those are the *indicator lamps* to monitor the control of the voltage.

—That's—

—Uh huh, she said. It's for fucking.

And from a small cardboard box lying on its side on the faded and dirty Indian rug *she produced the combination vaginal plug and cock ring attachment.* The attachment was made of a sturdy and durable transparent plastic, and, like the finest Steuben sculptures with their hints of silver and gold sunken in the glass renderings, the wires in the attachment, those glorious conductors, were glimmering in the plug and the ring. Yvonne had batteries in the device—it was running on battery power—and she juiced it up with the knobs and held the probe by the end.

—How are you going to use this for the movie? he said. You're going to get friends to use this and—

—Just touch your finger to it quickly. It's on the lowest setting.

—What the *fuck*? *Where did you get this?*

—I borrowed it. I'm thinking we should—

—Oh no, Randy said. If you think I'm gonna let you electrocute me with that thing, so that you can . . .

She touched it herself. Touched an index finger to it. There was a velocity to the way she was avoiding *the question in the air*. He had come over to talk about her pregnancy, to talk about the future, to raise practical questions, but instead they were here with the electrostimulator. There was a velocity, a speed and a direction, to her avoidance. She was using the device—that facsimile of the most potent Latin American political torture machines—to stray from *the implications of things*. And she wasn't foolish: she knew what she was doing. She touched the plug and he could hear its faint buzz, its melancholy hum. She held her finger there.

He took the thing from her and set it aside.

—Hey, Yvonne, Randy said. I got a more important question. That's why I came over here. I came over here to ask you something.

The plug snapped and fizzled on the edge of Yvonne's comforter.

—I came over here to ask you to marry me. That's what I came to do, Yvonne. We could get around this *problem* in a way you're probably not thinking of. The baby, I mean. We could just get married.

And he had the engagement ring, in his pocket, an antique silver band that had been in the family for a while. Impulsively, though, before taking the ring out of the tangle of khaki trousers on the floor, he took the cock ring from the electrostimulator and *set it on her ring finger.* She laughed. A nervous, high, piccolo laughter. He reached for the "course" knob.

—No way, she said. I'm too young to get married. I'm not carrying your fucking little *junior* around for nine months and fucking up my body and my hormones so that you'll have a peg to hang your hat on or someone to take care of you when you get senile. I don't want to spend my life with anybody, I can't even think of what my life will be like next week. I can't even imagine that I'll *have* a life next week. *Forget it.* Honey. Forget it.

Randy got really angry. He turned the stimulator all the way up. She laughed again. He brushed the device off the bed. They started to shout. They actually threw some stuff, some books and lamps, what kind of relationship was this, and what was she going to do, let this bad luck drive the last bit of fun out of their relationship when it could make them closer, and didn't she want to share anything with him, didn't she want to know that even on the lowest day she wasn't alone, didn't she want to wrinkle with someone around who loved her, didn't she want to file a joint tax return? But she wouldn't do it, wouldn't do it, wouldn't do it, and he couldn't believe that he had been so stupid that he thought this woman who sold hash and claimed she was some kind of filmmaker, that this woman was going to do this marriage-and-family thing with him, how could he be so stupid, and then they were fucking again and in the middle of these attentions some key of persuasion was turned in the lock and she was able to convince Randy that the electric stimulation device was an adventure, a gamble, a temporary shelter. In the penumbra of rejection he agreed to it. That was the decision that came first. In that penumbra, in the penumbra of late night, she had the tape player on and she had *the fine adjustment* on the stimulator control panel turned down as low as it would go and she had the video camera turned on, she had swiveled it on the tripod to take a closeup on Randy's face, and she put the cock ring around him now, though his cock was only halfway hard, and then she turned the knob up slowly. It was just like being drilled by the dentist at first, it was that sensation of wrong, of inappropriateness, and then there was a white alarm in his head as she turned it up and the sound of the capacitor inside dampening it and then the device scorched him like there were electromagnetic teeth ripping into his dick and he tore the thing off with the urgency that one shoos away an ornery wasp that has already deposited its venom and he collapsed on her bed for a second to catch his breath, to let the shock disperse itself throughout him. It was as though he were joining his friends the sleepwalkers as they too were bent upon the rack, *the rack of reactivity,* desperate simply for sensation in a monochromatic and decontextualized city. Yeah, it was right that he be here in this way, with the Ruin only a couple of nights behind him, with his fascination for the sleepwalkers and the transvestites and the perfect toes of the women at the bars. And he waited for the voltage to fade in him, until its absence was a sort of pleasure a sort of relief, and then he noticed her arm around him over his back and her voice in his ear saying *okay, okay,* that's right it seemed she was agreeing suddenly, she was changing her mind, *okay, okay,* yes she really was, *okay,* and so marriage was an interim government between them, and you could say all this lifelong and ever after stuff, but if it didn't work they could throw in the towel. She loved him in this vulnerable tableau with the electro-stimulation box beside him. She loved him. They would work it out. The kid would work it out. They would have the kid and the kid would understand that she had other ambitions. The kid would figure it out. Kids were like Superballs or something, like high-concentration rubber objects. Kids could learn to adjust. *Okay.* She lit the pipe. She toked on it. She passed it to him. Now it was her turn. She handed him the vaginal plug and lay back against the pillows.

Their marriage consisted of a civil ceremony on Staten Island, where the line at the courthouse was shorter. A friend of Yvonne's, Mike, filmed it, though none the footage worked, really. It was nothing she could use, except for a brief shot of the justice of the peace straightening his tie.

The Whiteness of Bones

Susanna Moore has written four novels, My Old Sweetheart, The Whiteness of Bones, Sleeping Beauty, *and* In the Cut. *Her lush, fragrant, and vividly sensuous prose reflects her native Hawaii. There is a poetic, haunting dreamlike quality to her explorations of passion, power, and loss. Her best work is eloquent, alluring, and disturbing.*

SHE ROSE IN THE BATHTUB, THE WATER STREAMING FROM her, puffs of soap bubbles, like clouds, clinging to her body.

He was at the door. He turned back into the room and took a towel and began to dry her back and waist, and the tops of her legs. When he reached the backs of her knees, the end of the towel fell into the water, so he gave her his hand, the second time that day over water, and she stepped out of the tub.

"This is going to be very interesting," he said, not looking at her, intent on drying her shoulders and stomach.

"What?"

"This. From now on."

He sat her down in the chair and took one of her feet in the towel to dry it. He was very thorough, drying between the toes and rubbing the heel. He dried the other foot. It was only when he finished and had put the towel aside on the wood floor where he was kneeling, that he looked at her face. She was the color of a pink rose, and her skin was porous and faintly swollen from the heat and the moisture.

He slowly pulled her knees apart so that her thighs were against the sides of the chair. He opened her gently with his fingers and looked at her.

She tried to close her legs, but he took her knees in both his hands and held them against the chair. She tried again to conceal herself, but this time he pushed her legs open with sudden, even impatient, firmness and he bent over her and put his mouth on her.

She did not want to watch him, even though she knew that what he was doing to her and what he was giving her were the very things that she and Lily Shields used to wonder about when they studied their vaginas, each in a separate room.

The sensation that began in her clitoris, of frustration and tension and startling pleasure, spread quickly through her body. She could feel the blood moving through her arteries, away from her strong heart, straight to his mouth. She could feel the electricity gathering slowly in every eager nerve. She could feel the slide of liquid between her buttocks and she did not know if it had come from her or if it was his saliva.

She made herself watch him. He took her hips in his hands, her knees splayed now in slack submission, and he tilted her hips so that she was more exposed to him and more open. He moved her hips back and forth in the chair.

"Do this," he said. "Slowly."

"I don't know what to do," she whispered.

"I'll tell you. I'll show you." He moved her with his hands until she caught the motion and began to move herself. She closed her eyes, afraid to let him see her.

"Breathe," he said. "You aren't breathing."

She didn't answer, pressing herself against him as if she could not draw him deep enough inside of her. She put her hands on his head and held him to her.

Later, when he kissed her on the mouth, she could taste and smell herself on him, and to her surprise and delight, it tasted and smelled like the sea.

Jazz

Toni Morrison was born in Lorain, Ohio, and educated at Howard University and Cornell. She has written six novels, Tar Baby, Song of Solomon, which won the 1978 National Book Critics Circle Award, Sula, The Bluest Eye, Beloved, which won the 1988 Pulitzer Prize, and Jazz. She was awarded the Nobel Prize for literature in 1993. She is the Robert F. Coneen Professor, Council of the Humanities, Princeton University.

THERE WAS AN EVENING, BACK IN 1906, BEFORE JOE AND Violet went to the City, when Violet left the plow and walked into their little shotgun house, the heat of the day still stunning. She was wearing coveralls and a sleeveless faded shirt and slowly removed them along with the cloth from her head. On a table near the cookstove stood an enamel basin, speckled blue and white and chipped all round its rim. Under a square of toweling, placed there to keep insects out, the basin was full of still water. Palms up, fingers leading, Violet slid her hands into the water and rinsed her face. Several times she scooped and splashed until, perspiration and water mixed, her cheeks and forehead cooled. Then, dipping the toweling into the water, carefully she bathed. From the windowsill she took a white shift, laundered that very morning, and dropped it over her head and shoulders. Finally she sat on the bed to unwind her hair. Most of the knots fixed that morning had loosened under her headcloth and were now cupfuls of soft wool her fingers thrilled to. Sitting there, her hands deep in the forbidden pleasure of her hair, she noticed she had not removed her heavy work shoes. Putting the toe of her left foot to the heel of the right, she pushed the shoe off. The effort seemed extra and the mild surprise at how very tired she felt was interrupted by a soft, wide hat, as worn and dim as the room she sat in, descending on her. Violet did not feel her shoulder touch the mattress. Way before that she had entered a safe sleep. Deep, trustworthy, feathered in colored dreams. The beat was relentless, insinuating. Like the voices of the women in houses nearby singing "Go down, go down, way down in Egypt land . . ." Answering each other from yard to yard with a verse or its variation.

Joe had been away for two months at Crossland, and when he got home and stood in the doorway, he saw Violet's dark girl-body limp on the bed. She looked frail to him, and penetrable everyplace except at one foot, the left, where her man's work shoe remained. Smiling, he took off his straw hat and sat down at the bottom of the bed. One of her hands held her face; the other rested on her thigh. He looked at the fingernails hard as her palm skin, and noticed for the first time how shapely her hands were. The arm that curved out of the shift's white sleeve was muscled by field labor, awful thin, but smooth as a child's. He undid the laces of her shoe and eased it off. It must have helped something in her dream for she laughed then, a light happy laugh that he had never heard before, but which seemed to belong to her.

"Old Budapest"

Joyce Carol Oates has written twenty-five novels and twenty short story collections as well as numerous volumes of poetry, essays, and plays. Her variety and complexity are staggering. She is a boldly original spinner of tales who is totally unique in her relentless and deeply insightful probing of America's dark side.

SHE HEARD LAUGHTER FROM THE OTHER ROOM.

She was ready to return with her various lemon slices when someone entered the kitchen behind her. She heard the floorboards gently creaking; but no one spoke. It might be Tommy playfully tiptoeing up behind her . . . it might be the deputy chief of mission come to see what was taking her so long . . . it might be the cultural attaché on an errand, sent to fetch more Brazil nuts (the men had been eating them rather gluttonously) or cocktail napkins. Marianne didn't turn but she saw a tall ghostly reflection in an aluminum door to one of the cupboards: tall: which (fortunately) ruled out the director of public relations who was hardly more than her height. She couldn't identify the man but she chose not to turn in surprise; instead she pretended to be cutting a final lemon slice, nervously aware of her pretty small-boned hands . . . and her perfect fingernails which were painted a pale frosted pink . . . and her numerous rings and bracelets (perhaps she wore too many but she loved them all: each item of jewelry was distinctive, each represented a certain pinnacle of achievement, gifts from admirers, gifts from Marianne to herself, the exquisite white-gold Swiss watch with diamonds for numerals . . . the opal ring edged with sapphires . . . the antique pearl ring . . . and the rest). She continued to hum to herself as the anonymous man approached her from behind. He was making no effort to walk softly, he wasn't trying to alarm or surprise her, it might be said to be a romantic gesture, gracefully executed.

The first kiss would be delicate as a bone-china teacup of the kind one might unwittingly crush between his fingers, holding it too tight.

The man slid his arm lightly across her shoulders. And may have murmured a question. Marianne shivered with pleasure at the very casualness of his touch. She might have been a wife, he might have been a husband, how fragrant the lilacs blooming in the sunshine just outside the window, how tart, how bracing, the smell of fresh-cut lemon, and her hands *were* beautiful, and her rings and bracelets and her black silk blouse and designer suits. . . . Marianne drew a breath of sheer exhilaration that she was the very person she was: Marianne Beecher and no one else.

Perhaps it was only Tommy after all, Marianne thought as she lay the paring knife carefully down, and wiped her fingers on a napkin. (He had playfully nuzzled her neck in the back of the embassy limousine while they were being driven here, after their long giddy lunch; but they were not yet lovers, he was being presumptuous, from Marianne's pragmatic point of view it wasn't completely settled that they would become lovers.) It might well be the deputy chief of mission, whose kitchen this was, after all, and whose rank was very high: just below Ambassador. Yet what if it was the mysterious Michel with his curt clipped manner and his reluctant smile. . . . She hoped it was not the cultural attaché who was clearly a very nice bright hard-working man but too earnest for Marianne's taste, and of a rank she found difficult to take seriously.

He gripped her shoulder; Marianne instinctively closed her eyes, and rested her head back against him as they kissed; and immediately she felt a splendid rush of emotion, hazy, sweet, familiar, she was sixteen years old, she was fourteen, even thirteen, being kissed in a doorway . . . being kissed surreptitiously at a party . . . breathless in a corner, her heart beating hard, her eyes shut. . . . She might have been even younger, ten or eleven, practicing kisses against the mirror in her bedroom, secret and daring.

It was a gentle kiss, experimental, improvised. Marianne responded with a small frisson of surprise, a semblance of surprise. She was touching his arm lightly, she hoped she had wiped off the lemon juice, how sweet to be approached with such tact and delicacy, in so gentlemanly a fashion, she thought suddenly of the Hungarian editor and herself walking on Gellert Hill, and along the Danube, the warm moist sunshine heavy with the smell of lilacs, so many romantic couples, lovers, the young ones amorous as puppies, but there were middle-aged lovers too, Marianne was embarrassed to see a man and a woman in their fifties, pressed close together on a stone bench, kissing with such frank and impassioned energy that they must have been oblivious of their surroundings . . . and Ottó said in an undertone, Romance is desperation and we are a desperate people—we laugh a great deal too.

Now she felt the kiss deepen, and a feathery-light sensation ran through her body, her belly, her loins, a sensation familiar enough but always in a way new, and reassuring, and impersonal; and in another second or two the tenor of the kiss would change and become more serious: the man would part her lips, his tongue would prod at hers, his teeth grind lightly against hers, they would still be smiling but the kiss would have become serious, and Marianne's plans for the rest of the day—was this Saturday?—might have to be substantially altered.

GWENDOLYN M. PARKER

These Same Long Bones

Gwendolyn M. Parker gave up her career on Wall Street to devote herself to writing. Her debut novel, These Same Long Bones, *is that rare thing today, a warm-hearted and moving work whose intelligence and insight match its generosity of spirit.*

"AILIE," SIRUS SAID, BUT AILEEN DIDN'T HEAR HIM. HE TRIED gently to pull her hands away from her face, and then tried to move her legs from her chest, but Aileen resisted, and as he tried harder, she pulled herself tighter. So they stayed like that, their tensions and strengths equal, neither moving, until Sirus took his hands away and let them hover above her, stroking the space between them. He poured all of his love into that space, using everything these painful days had forced him to know, and he circled her around with his love, which was open to heartache, and cruelty, even death, stroking the air between them, around and around, slowly, ever so slowly, closer and closer, until just his fingers brushed her skin, feathering across her. He trailed one finger slowly after the other, and soon, as she let him, his touch grew a little stronger, so that he was stroking her, then kneading her skin, then taking her face in his hands. He cupped his hands over hers on her face. "Ailie, look at me," he said.

She let her hands drop and slowly looked up. In her husband's face she recognized the child they had birthed together and had lost.

"You're so soft," she said, and as she said it, she suddenly knew it was true. As she looked at him, she saw, as if she had never seen him before, that he was as soft as she was, not at all strong the way she'd always imagined, but soft at the center, soft at the center of his eyes, at the center of his heart, where anything and everything could pierce him, just as things pierced her, and his strength was just muscle and bone that shielded his soft heart.

"Hold me," she said, and Sirus took her into his arms. He held her against his chest, where she could hear his heart beating, and she wrapped her arms around his chest and up to where she could stroke his face. She could feel the pulse behind his ear and he could feel her breasts against him and she could feel his breath in her hair and he could feel her eyelids moving across his chest. They held on to each other, each melting into the other, all the grief and the anger and the reserve and the guilt melting, until there was nothing left in either of them but a hole into which they were both opening.

"You loved our child, Ailie," Sirus said.

Neither of them moved. They kept their arms tight around each other until the sun came up, each falling slowly, deeper and deeper, closer and closer to the center of the other's heart.

Martin and John

When Martin and John *was published in 1993, Michael Cunningham said Dale Peck's uniquely original voice was "like an angel chewing on rope and glass." The novel, a boldly conceived work full of elegance and energy, mystery and sadness, possesses a lyrical solemnity that is deeply moving.*

SOMETIMES SEX IS PERFECT. I REMEMBER MY FOURTH TIME with Martin, the first time we fucked. I remember the fourth time because that's when I fell for him. Something held us back our first three times; our minds were elsewhere, our hands could have been tied. But the fourth time. There we were: Martin's place, Martin's old couch. There we were: Martin and John. The two of us, 3 A.M., empty bottles on the coffee table. We had exhausted conversation, wine had exhausted us, we stared at the TV. It was turned off. How did he do it? I mean, I know what he did: he put his hand on my leg. He didn't look at me when he did it, just lifted his right hand off his right leg and set it down on my left one, just above my knee. Just above my knee, and then it slid up my thigh, slowly, but not wasting time. That's what he did. But how did he make my diaphragm contract so tightly that I couldn't take one breath for the entire minute it took his hand to move to my belt? My stomach was so tight a penny would have bounced off it. His fingers found the belt buckle, worked it, a small sound of metal on metal, a sudden release, a rush of air — my lungs' air — and my pants were open and I gasped for breath.

Martin put his hand back in his lap. His words, when they came, were even. He could have been talking about the weather. You could slip a condom on your cock, he said, and twirl me on it like a globe on its axis. The words took shape in the room; they made sex seem as understandable as pornography. On the blank TV screen I imagined I saw Martin and myself, fucking. I looked down at my open pants, at my underwear, white as a sheet of paper. Or I could do you, he said. Still, I hesitated, not because I didn't want him, but because the very thought of fucking Martin added so many possibilities to my life that I grew dizzy contemplating them. Just do what you want to do, Martin said, but do it now. I kissed him. I pulled open the buttons of his shirt, pushed down his pants. I bent over him and ran my tongue over his chest, into his navel, down to his cock and balls. When I got there I swabbed the shaft until it glistened. I rolled his balls around my mouth the way a child rolls marbles in his hand. And it's important to know that I didn't do this because I suddenly loved him. I just wanted to fuck. Do it, I whispered. Do it.

And he did, lying on the floor, on a rug, though I didn't twirl as easily as those globes in high school, and in fact, after one revolution, I didn't twirl at all, but sat astride him and rocked up and down. And he pumped, pumped like anyone in any skinflick ever made, though I didn't think of that then, but only of the amazing sensation of having this man inside me. A funny thing happened then. He pumped and I rocked, and I rocked and he pumped, and eventually our rhythm must have been just right, for the rug, a small Persian carpet–type thing patterned in tangled growing vines, came out from under us as if it had been pulled. I fell over, he slipped out of me, we ended up on our sides, side by side, laughing. We lay on the floor for a long time, mouths open, our stomachs heaving as we sucked in air. We touched each other only with our fingertips, and then only slightly, and we lay on the floor for a long time, laughing.

We finished on his bed. I don't remember going there, just a point at which the world returned like a shadow and I saw my cum splashed on his stomach and legs, and his splashed on mine, and below us was a white sheet instead of the rug. Then for a moment I wanted to take everything a step further. I wanted to run my finger through Martin's cum and lick the finger clean. But Martin smiled at me. He kissed me. When my hands went for his body, he caught them halfway and held them. In a light voice he said, In my experience, there are two kinds of men in the world: those who play with their lover's hair when they're getting a blowjob, and those who play with their own. Though I tried, I couldn't remember what I'd done. Which type am I? I asked. You, he said, and showed me as he told me, put one hand on my head, and one on yours. And which are you? Martin looked at my hair. If there was a mirror handy, he said, you wouldn't have to ask that question. His words didn't really *mean* anything, but they accomplished what I think he meant them to: I forgot my desire to taste his cum. He lifted the sheet then and fluffed it with his arms, like wings, then let it settle on our shoulders, and I didn't realize we were standing up until I awoke hours later.

After that he could have asked me to do anything. A caress from Martin had more strength than any punch Henry would ever land. But he rarely used this power, and I suppose I had the same control over him. Didn't he, as well, sleep standing in my arms? We shut the windows, turned off the phone, unplugged the clock. We wore no clothes for days, and used our time to make love, to eat and sleep. What I remember from that time, the time we shut out the world, is sweating on his bed as he dove into me, and someone somewhere flushing a toilet and the wall behind Martin's bed rattling as water rushed through pipes concealed within it.

The Professor of Desire

Philip Roth's work and career has been one of the cosmic phenomena of the twentieth century, providing even face-shaped-rocks-seen-on-Mars fodder for the tabloids. If there had never been a Philip Roth, it would have been necessary to invent one. Born in New Jersey in 1933 and educated at Bucknell and at the University of Chicago, Roth's books have been major literary events almost from the beginning, with the publication of Goodbye, Columbus *in 1959. His satire on modern Jewish-American life,* Portnoy's Complaint, *was considered revolting by nearly everyone who failed to see it as satire. Yet, it remains one of the great visceral explorations of modern life. Every once in a while, he emerges from the internal labyrinths of mind and emotion and visits the world of the physical. In his deft hands, that world is as physical as any world ever gets. His novel* The Professor of Desire *was considered by many an abberation in his literary ouvre, something to do with turmoils in his personal life. One could only hope the same may be said of all his work.*

"OH, GOD," SAYS HELEN, STRETCHING LANGUOROUSLY when morning comes, "fucking is such a lovely thing to do."

True, true, true, true, true. The passion is frenzied, inexhaustible, and in my experience, singularly replenishing. Looking back to Birgitta, it seems to me, from my new vantage point, that we were, among other things, helping each other at age twenty-two to turn into something faintly corrupt, each the other's slave and slaveholder, each the arsonist and the inflamed. Exercising such strong sexual power over each other, *and* over total strangers, we had created a richly hypnotic atmosphere, but one which permeated the inexperienced *mind* first of all: I was intrigued and exhilarated at least as much by the idea of what we were engaged in as by the sensations, what I felt and what I saw. Not so with Helen. To be sure, I must first accustom myself to what strikes me at the height of my skepticism as so much theatrical display; but soon, as understanding grows, as familiarity grows, and feeling with it, I begin at last to relinquish some of my suspiciousness, to lay off a little with my interrogations, and to see these passionate performances as arising out of the very fearlessness that so draws me to her, out of that determined abandon with which she will give herself to whatever strongly beckons, and regardless of how likely it is to bring in the end as much pain as pleasure. I have been dead wrong, I tell myself, trying to dismiss hers as a corny and banalized mentality deriving from *Screen Romance*—rather, she is *without* fantasy, there is no *room* for fantasy, so total is her concentration, and the ingenuity with which she sounds her desire. Now, in the aftermath of orgasm, I find myself weak with gratitude and the profoundest feelings of self-surrender. I am the least guarded, if not the simplest, organism on earth. I don't even know what to say at such moments. Helen does, however. Yes, there are the things that this girl knows and knows and knows. "I love you," she tells me. Well, if something has to be said, what makes more sense? So we begin to tell each other that we are lovers who are in love, even while my conviction that we are on widely divergent paths is revived from one conversation to the next. Convinced as I would like to be that a kinship, rare and valuable, underlies and nourishes our passionate rapport, I still cannot wish away the grand uneasiness Helen continues to arouse. Why else can't we stop—can't *I* stop—the fencing and the parrying?

"Plaisir D'Amour"

Lynne Sharon Schwartz was born in Brooklyn, New York, and educated at Barnard and Bryn Mawr. She has written seven works of fiction. Her first novel, Rough Strife, *written in 1980, was nominated both for an American Book Award and for a PEN/Hemingway First Book Award.* Leaving Brooklyn *(1989), a lyrical, vivid, and compelling tale of female rite of passage, is perhaps her best-known work. Her work is an unmistakable blend of intellectual precision, grace, wit, sadness, and sex. Her writing tends to focus on individualities of perception and vision—both literally and as a metaphor for the individual's relation to the external world. This excerpt is from her short story "Plaisir D'Amour," about a romantic couple invented in the mind of a lonely widow, which appeared in her excellent 1984 collection,* Acquainted with the Night.

SHE WAS JUST FALLING ASLEEP WHEN SHE SENSED THAT Brauer and Elemi were in the room. Strange, she had not noticed them enter. Brauer had his hands on Elemi's shoulders. He pulled her towards him, clasped her tightly, and kissed her long on the mouth. Vera was surprised, and a trifle amused. Aha, she thought. So they are not such innocents. Elemi's arms closed around Brauer and she began caressing his back. Brauer bent and buried his face in her neck, roughly, and Elemi, her eyes closed, leaned her head back and gasped. Her fingers were taut and clutching at him. Vera's eyes began to pound. No, she thought in panic. Not yet. But they didn't stop. They sank down to the floor, where Brauer helped Elemi pull off her shirt, then put his lips to her breast. Elemi had her small white hand on the inside of his thigh. Vera shut her eyes tight but the vision remained. There was no way to get rid of them. Not yet, she tried to scream, but no sound would come. She felt herself grow inflamed, blood pounding and rushing to every surface. You want to see it, she whispered angrily. You know you want to see it. Yes, all along she had secretly wondered why, if they were so in love, they never made love. They must have done it behind her back, like naughty children. Why were they showing her now? Why now, she wanted to scream at them. But of course they would not hear. The pounding of her blood was unbearable. Her eyes were hot and every inch of her skin ached as she watched, for now they were intertwined in another long kiss, arms and legs groping, seizing. Vera placed a hand beneath her heart to calm herself, but the warm touch only made the throbbing worse. If it kept on she would soon burst from her skin.

Furious at herself, she snarled, If you want to see it so badly then take a good look. They were completely naked now. Vera cried out in fright—Brauer was so strong and hard, Elemi so white and frail. His fingers disappeared between her legs; Vera's spine jerked in a spasm of terror. Elemi seemed nearly faint in her abandon. In the park so pretty and childlike, now she had her legs spread apart, with her arms clinging around Brauer's neck and her open lips reaching for his. Then he was on top of her. Vera stiffened. Don't hurt Elemi, she whispered. Don't. Don't hurt. He began to push. She could see Elemi's face very clearly, the tight tendons of her arched neck, the trembling bluish-white of her eyelids, her mouth open as if in shock. Sweat glistened on Elemi's forehead. Brauer kept pushing, merciless, rhythmic. Elemi's face was so strained and twisted, Vera could not tell if it was misery or joy. Her own body began moving up and down in rhythm with Brauer's pushing and she could not stop it. No, not yet, she cried, but she was powerless to stop herself or them. They had escaped her. She had escaped herself.

On and on Brauer pushed—would he never stop? Vera ached to know what Elemi was feeling, poor Elemi, straining with him, pounding up and down on the floor so hard her frail body made a soft thudding sound. Was that wild face twisted in misery or joy? Somewhere within her she remembered that Elemi could feel only what she wished her to feel, yet Vera was powerless, caught in their unstoppable rhythm, for she could not choose between misery or joy. Brauer kept pushing, and Elemi's face kept the terrible riddle, till Vera herself finally erupted from the inside out, shattering the air around her.

When it was finished she leaned back weakly and wiped her streaming brow with the back of her hand, amazed to have survived. Her body was utterly limp and exhausted, but when she focused her eyes she saw that they, the dream, strained on. Still he pushed without respite and still she thudded beneath him. They would never stop.

Playing with Fire

Dani Shapiro received an MFA in creative writing from Sarah Lawrence College. She is the author of three novels, Playing with Fire, Fugitive Fire, *and* Picturing the Wreck. *She lives in New York City and teaches creative writing at both Columbia University and the graduate program at New York University. This excerpt from* Playing with Fire, *like all her work, is a complex exploration about the intertwining of passion and pain in familial life.*

I DECIDE TO TAKE A SHOWER IN THE BATHROOM DOWN THE hall. There are two shower stalls, six toilets and four sinks. I pad down the corridor in my new silk robe, a Chanukah present from my mother. In my arms I hold soft pink towels which smell like home.

The trickles of water make their way slowly down my up-turned face. The water pressure here is almost nonexistent, but it is hot, so I stand still, inhaling the steam. I unwrap the almond-scented soap which I charged to my father's account at the drugstore (along with candles, massage oil and body lotion), and make figure eights around my stomach with its smooth, waxy surface.

I am enjoying having the big bathroom all to myself. I shake my hair, sending drops of water flying. I pull a towel around me, absorbing moisture. I look in the mirror. I have lost weight in the last few months. My legs are thin, and my rear end, which has never been my strong point, is high and firm. I can count my ribs, which I do. I have six on each side.

When Carolyn walks in, I am standing like a stork by the sink, one leg lifted high onto the basin, shaving. She stands watching in the doorway.

"Don't stop on my account," she says, "I should go get my camera."

"Why?" I stop, razor poised in midair.

"You look like an advertisement for shaving cream, or towels, or college bathrooms," she smiles at me, still standing there. "You do wonders for all three."

Her leather suitcase sits by her feet, and a tote bag is slung over one shoulder. She has a new haircut, soft layers falling around her face, framing her cheekbones, making her large, dark eyes seem even wider than before. Of course, she is tan. I have rarely seen Carolyn without a tan. It is as if she was born in the sun. She is wearing a light yellow sweater and tight faded jeans tucked into impractical suede boots.

"Come back to the room," she tells me, and walks away. She has not come over to give me a hug, to kiss me, to say hello. After she leaves, I quickly finish shaving, nicking myself in the process. I encircle my neck with the wet towel, and wrap my robe around me as I make my way back up the hall.

When I walk in the door, she is standing there with camera in hand.

"Take off your beautiful new robe," she says quickly, quietly.

I untie the sash, and my robe falls like a whisper to the floor. I am more naked than I've ever been. My nipples grow hard in the cold, and something deep in my stomach contracts. With one slender finger Carolyn wipes the last bit of shaving cream from behind my knee.

She places her antique quilt over the armchair, arranging it so that the folds hang in even ripples.

"Sit down," she commands me in the same low voice. She chooses a lens from her camera case, twisting it until it snaps into place.

I sit on the edge of the chair, my legs crossed, hands folded over my breasts. My hair lies wet on my back.

"Lucy, that isn't sitting. That's posing. Relax," she tells me, standing in the center of the room.

She adjusts the light, moving the scented candle over to a small table next to my chair. I ease back, feeling the curve of the seat underneath me. The quilt smells like Carolyn: a combination of Shalimar and Ivory soap.

The only sound in the room is that of the shutter clicking. I begin to loosen, layers falling away easily, carelessly, like a child opening a box full of tissue paper, eager to get at the core. I am amazed that I'm comfortable like this, my arms falling to my sides, Carolyn crouched on one knee, shooting up at me. My thoughts seem to come to me through a distant mist; they are diluted. I think everything is fine, finer than it has ever been.

Click. My legs are crossed at the thigh, my arms resting on either side of the armchair. I look down. My breasts seem to float above my rib cage, as buoyant as if they were resting on water. I close my eyes, tilting my head until it falls all the way back. *Click.* I lift one arm above my head, angling it, exposing a freshly shaved armpit. I swivel slightly, jutting one hip slightly toward the camera, toward Carolyn. *Click.* I raise my other arm, cradling my head with both hands. I keep my eyes closed. This is my world: this heat, this quiet, this darkness. I hear the whir of the camera closer to my face. She is to one side of me, then to the other, then directly in front of me. I don't want to see her face. I don't want her to see mine. There is a camera between us, a mechanical, impartial witness, in black and white.

I sink deeper. I think about the day I met her, the firm, cool handshake, the level gaze, the same gaze which is now leveled at me. I think of the train ride, her damp head against my shoulder, the way she held me outside the brownstone on East Sixty-first Street. "I'll be with you," she told me that day. "Nothing will hurt you," she said. "Everything will be all right."

Weekends she is gone without a trace. Many nights her bed remains untouched. Whole weeks she disappears, returning with a tan, always laughing, "No, I'm not tan," eyes looking directly into mine, defiant, never giving in.

She has secrets. She understands the nature of silence. She knows how to hide, and how never to be found.

The clicking stops. Carolyn is inches away from me. She is kneeling in front of me. I feel her breath on my shins. I begin to shake, an uncontrollable shudder which begins with my toes and spreads upward until my whole body is moving independently, and I can no longer tell it what to do.

"Lucy, look at me." Her voice is trembling. I keep my eyes closed. I see a sort of triptych of purple and blue. My mind's eye absorbs me with its shifting colors. The only undeviating element is the black line running down the middle. There are two distinct sides.

"Open your eyes," she asks me. She is so near that she only has to whisper. I feel her hair brushing my knee.

"I can't," I say. I am in a perfect, weightless moment, a precipice, balanced between going forward and looking back. I am dead center between the purple and blue, the black and white. I am in the middle of the triptych. I want to stay like this, sitting on the line, straddling the fence.

"Why?" She kisses the inside of one knee, gently parting them with her mouth.

"I don't know . . ."

I'm stalling. I want to remain here, in this hour before life shifts imperceptibly, hanging in the balance.

Her tongue is soft. She is tracing a wet line up my thigh. Her hands touch my hipbones, then move higher.

"Carolyn, this can't happen." My voice comes out in a whisper, in a croak.

"Why?"

She doesn't believe me. She is used to getting her way. Her fingers encircle my nipples, which are now hard for reasons other than the cold January air.

I moan. I shake. My hips rise and fall. In one more second I will have no choice in the matter.

"Carolyn, this isn't going to happen."

I force open my eyes. The black line disappears. She looks up at me from between my legs. Her eyes are moist, and her mouth is moister. She is still wearing her light yellow sweater, tight jeans and knee-high suede boots. I am wearing gold hoops in my ears, and a Timex on my wrist.

I focus on the room, its familiar outlines falling into place. The scented candle has filled the air with jasmine. Carolyn sits cross-legged on the floor, her cheek against the side of the chair. I stroke her head, my fingers gliding easily through the layers of her new haircut. She is staring out the window, into the gathering dusk. The fading sunlight casts red shadows across her face. Between us, her camera lies, black and mechanical, like a bomb.

I cover myself with my robe, tying the sash in a double bow. I try to run a comb through my hair, but it is matted from the previous hour. Carolyn comes up behind me.

"Bird's nests?" she asks with her same old smile.

I hand her the comb.

"This may hurt," she tells me, gathering up a few strands of hair at a time, carefully unknotting them.

It doesn't hurt. I don't feel a thing. When she is finished, I turn around. I look at her, I keep my eyes on hers as I move closer and closer to her face.

"Don't close your eyes," I murmur.

She is perfectly still. With every inch, her eyes seem wider.

I see flecks of green and gold the instant before I feel her eyelashes on mine, the instant before I kiss her.

The first thing I notice is an absence of stubble. Her cheeks are as smooth and cold as marble. Her tongue feels strangely like my own. I hold her head in both hands as I explore her mouth. We stand like this, eyes open, too close to see anything at all.

I love her. This sentence, the smallest of sentences, forms in my head so clearly that for a terrifying moment I wonder whether I've said it out loud. I look at her, soft and unfocused, and realize that I haven't. I am grateful for this, because I have no idea what these particular words, in this particular context, can possibly mean.

Touch

Charlotte Watson Sherman is the author of two novels, One Dark Body *and* Touch, *as well as* Killing Color, *a collection of short stories. She is also a widely published poet and the editor of* Sisterfire: Black Womanist Fiction and Poetry. *Her work is warm, sensuous, magical, and moving. This excerpt is from chapter 15 of* Touch.

MARCH 12, 1994

I told Theodore I was positive last night. On the Ferris wheel. At the top of the world. He was more afraid of the height than what I had to tell him.

His brother died of AIDS.

Sheila calls what Theodore has "survivor's guilt." Theodore has always felt guilty. His work with Mrs. Jenkins and her Dancing Unicorn House kids helps him with that. But I can't help wondering, How do you look into the eyes of a dying child and stay sane?

Theodore wants to keep seeing me.

When we got back to my apartment, I lit my candles and

we sat on the area rug on the living room floor. Theodore took off his coat, but left the rest of his clothes on. I had on my denim skirt and black tights. My sweater without a bra.

We don't have to be afraid of loving, he said. This is not the time to be without touch, he said. Now is when we need it more than ever. And I'm not talking about sex, I'm talking about touch, he said.

He took my hands in his and kissed them. I started to feel afraid for him. He placed my hands on his face and shook his head until I stopped being afraid. He laid me down on the rug. He slipped off my shoes, pulled down my tights. He brushed his lips gently across my toes, then kissed each one. He raised my leg and brushed his mustache across my ankle, over the soles of my feet. His breath was hot when he blew on my calf. It tickled. He trailed his tongue along the inside of my thigh and I started to squirm.

You want me to stop? he asked.

What could I do but moan?

He ran his hands over my behind under my skirt, squeezing, kneading, caressing. He put his head under my skirt and planted kisses around the edges of my panties.

Wait, I said. Wait.

He stopped.

His lips had branded my skin. Don't stop, I said, remembering Sheila and Janice's encouraging words. I am alive and a sensual being. I am entitled to this pleasure.

I felt so alive beneath the warmth of his breath. His lips made me think about anything but death.

Theodore helped me remove my sweater. He traced circles

around my navel, then slid his tongue to my nipples where he took one, then the other, between his teeth. He kissed my stomach before he blew his breath on my neck. My legs began to shake.

Just a minute, he said.

I was still, but my body was making a sound something like humming.

Theodore returned with the Kama Sutra massage oil. Chocolate Mint. He opened it and told me to lie on my stomach. His hands smoothed the oil on my body, into my hungry skin. He held my calves, thighs, buttocks in his hands and stroked them, massaged my back until not one knot of tension remained. Easily, he rubbed my neck, pushed his tongue into my ear, rolled me over and massaged the front of my body, my thighs, my stomach, my breasts, my shoulders, and then when I was nothing but honey beneath his hands, he laid his body on top of me and we lay like that until I started to rub myself against him, against the rough texture of the pants that covered his muscled thigh, then I pushed myself against his body until he lay beneath me and I was astride him and able to ride until I reached a land where there was no AIDS, no terror, no secrets, only this grinding pleasure, this wicked wetness between my legs.

And that's just a taste of what safer sex can be like, he said.

We lay on that rug for hours breathing together, licking, rubbing, holding, being still. It was as if the HIV had broken something open in our relationship; there was no room for lying or secrets. There was not even space for promises. Those, I told him, are forbidden. He made me promise to meet Mrs.

Jenkins and her kids, though. So I will do it. For myself and for Theodore.

How could I say no to a man who can caress me with words like that?

⌁ JANE SMILEY ⌁

A Thousand Acres

Jane Smiley was born in Los Angeles and grew up in St. Louis. She studied at Vassar College and at the University of Iowa, where she received her Ph.D. She lives in—and writes about—Ames, Iowa. She is the author of such acclaimed works of fiction as The Age of Grief, *which was nominated for a National Book Critics Circle Award,* Ordinary Love, *and* A Thousand Acres, *for which she was awarded the Pulitzer Prize. This excerpt is from* A Thousand Acres, *her brilliant retelling of the* King Lear *story from the eldest daughter's point of view. She lives in Ames, Iowa.*

I LAY AWAKE IN THE HOT DARKNESS, NAKED AND COVERED by the sheet. Every so often, I lifted the sheet and looked under it, at my blue-white skin, my breasts, with their dark nipples, the foreshortened, rounded triangles of my legs, my jutting feet. I looked at myself while I thought about having sex with Jess Clark and I could feel my flesh turn electric at these thoughts, could feel sensation gather at my nipples, could feel my vagina relax and open, could feel my lips and my fingertips grow sensitive enough to know their own shapes. When I turned on my side and my breasts swam together and I flicked the sheet for a bit of air, I saw only myself turning, my same old shape moving in the same old way. I turned onto my stomach so that I wouldn't be able to look, so that I could bury my face in the black pillow. It wasn't like me to think such thoughts, and though they drew me, they repelled me too. I began to drift off, maybe to escape what I couldn't stop thinking about.

Ty, who was asleep, rolled over and put his hand on my shoulder, then ran it down my back, so slowly that my back came to seem about as long and humped as a sow's, running in a smooth arc from my rooting, low-slung head to my little stumpy tail. I woke up with a start and remembered the baby pigs. Ty was very close to me. It was still hot, and he was pressing his erection into my leg. Normally I hated waking in the night with him so close to me, but my earlier fantasies must have primed me, because the very sense of it there, a combination of feeling its insistent pressure and imagining its smooth heavy shape, doused me like a hot wave, and instantly I was breathless. I put my hand around it and turned toward it, then took my hand off it and pulled the curve of his ass toward me. But for once I couldn't stand not touching it, knowing it was there but not holding it in my hand. Ty woke up. I was panting, and he was on me in a moment. It was something: it was deeply exciting and simultaneously not enough. The part of me that was still a sow longed to wallow, to press my skin against his and be engulfed. Ty whispered, "Don't open your eyes," and I did not. Nothing would wake me from this unaccustomed dream of my body faster than opening my eyes.

Afterward, when we did open our eyes and were ourselves again, I saw that it was only ten-fifteen. I moved away, to the cooler edge of the bed. Ty said, "I liked that. That was nice," and he put his hand affectionately on my hip without actually looking at me. His voice carried just a single quiver of embarrassment. That was pretty good for us. Then I heard the breeze start up, rustling the curtains, and then I heard the rattle of hog feeders and the sound of a car accelerating in the distance. The moon was full, and the shadows of bats fluttered in the moonlight. The sawing of cicadas distinguished itself, the barking of a dog. I fell asleep.

With Jess Clark in that old pickup bed in the dump the next afternoon, it was much more awkward. My arms and legs, stiff and stalklike, thumped against the wheel well, the truck bed, poked Jess in the ribs, the back. My skin looked glaringly white, white like some underground sightless creature. When he leaned forward to untie his sneakers, I felt my cheeks. As clammy as clay. Jess eased me backward. I didn't watch while he unbuttoned my shirt. He said, "All right?"

I nodded.

"Really?"

"I'm not very used to this."

He pulled back, away from me, the look on his face unsmiling, suddenly cautious.

"Yes," I said. "Please." It was humiliating to ask, but that was okay, too. Reassuring in a way. He smiled. That was the reward.

Then, afterward, I began all at once to shiver.

He pulled away and I buttoned three buttons on my shirt. He said, "Are you cold? It's only ninety-four degrees out here."

"Maybe t-t-t-terrified."

But I wasn't, not anymore. Now the shaking was pure desire. As I realized what we had done, my body responded as it hadn't while we were doing it—hadn't ever done, I thought. I felt blasted with the desire, irradiated, rendered transparent. Jess said, "Are you okay?"

I said, "Hold me for a while, and keep talking."

He laughed a warm, pleasant, very intimate laugh and said something about let's see, well, the Sears man would be out tomorrow, at last, and I came in a drumming rush from toes to head. I buried some moans in his neck and shoulder, and he hugged me tightly enough to crack my ribs, which was just tightly enough to contain me. I thought. He kept talking. Harold was feeling a little sheepish, and making Loren tuna-and-mushroom-soup-with-noodles casserole for dinner. Jess had promised to put it in the oven at four-thirty; what time was it now? The farmer near Sac City had called him back, four hundred and seventy acres in corn and beans, only green manures and animal manures for fertilizer, the guy's name was Morgan Boone, which sounded familiar, did it sound familiar to me? He said Jess could come any time. Jess held me away from him again, and gazed at me for a long minute or two. I looked at the creases under his eyes, his beaky nose, his serious expression. His face was deeply familiar to me, as if I'd been staring at it my whole life. I took some deep breaths and lay back on his shoulder. The sky was steel blue, the sun caught in the lacy leaves of the locust trees above us. I wanted to say, what now, but that was a dangerous temptation for sure, so I didn't.

⊰ SUSAN SONTAG ⊱

The Volcano Lover

Essayist, philosopher, novelist, short-story writer, and film-maker Susan Sontag was born in New York City. She received a B.A. from the University of Chicago (graduating when she was eighteen) and an M.A. in both English and philosophy from Harvard. Her early essays on art and culture were collected in the influential volume, Against Interpretation (1966).

   In 1975 she was diagnosed with breast cancer. Her doctors were not optimistic. She was told she would not live. She underwent five operations, including a mastectomy, and several years of chemotherapy. These experiences led her to write Illness as Metaphor (1977). On Philosophy (1977) won a National Book Critics' Circle Award. A Susan Sontag Reader was published in 1981. Many critics consider her recent historical novel, The Volcano Lover (1992), from which this excerpt is taken, not only her finest work but also an extremely important contribution to contemporary American culture. Susan Sontag currently lives in Manhattan and is at work on a new novel.

THE CAVALIERE WAS CORRECT IN SUPPOSING THE GUESTS
had departed. Indeed, the servants had almost finished clean-
ing up in the great salon. His wife and their friend had gone
to their separate quarters, and then the Cavaliere's wife joined
the hero in his room at two in the morning. She had brought
him some figs of Barbary, pomegranates, and Sicilian cakes
covered with white sugar and lemon peel. She worried that he
did not eat enough, he was so thin, and that he slept so little.
Their hours together—usually from two until five in the morning, when she would return to her own quarters—were the
only time they could be alone; she could sleep late, but he
always rose at dawn. And they too stood on the balcony and
breathed in the warm air scented with laurel and blossoming
orange and almond trees, and admired the clouds that had
been lowered from heaven, steeped in orange and pink. But
there was no longing for what was absent or left behind. Everything was here, complete.

She loved to undress him, as if he were a child. He had the
most beautiful skin of any man she had known, soft as a girl's.
She pressed her lips to the poor scorched stump of his arm.
He flinched. She kissed it again. He sighed. She kissed his
groin and he laughed and pulled her onto the bed, into their
position—they already had habits. She lay her head on his
right shoulder, he held her with his left arm. That was the way
they always lay: it was so comforting. It is your place. Your
body is my arm.

She stroked his wavy hair, easing his head toward her so her
face could receive his breath. She touched his cheek, with its
beautiful stubble. She clasped him to her, her fingers scrib-

bling down his back, her palm sliding upward to erase it. Their languid lying side by side began to quicken. She threw her leg over his hip and locked him to her. He groaned, and fell into her body. The work of pleasure began: the drop and push of pelvis, bone sheathed in flesh dissolving, blooming into pure fall. How deep it was. Touch me here, she said. I want your mouth here. And here. Deeper. Pressing, squeezing, at first she had feared she might overwhelm him with the intensity of her desire for him; he seemed so fragile to her. But he wanted to be dominated by her, he wanted to be flooded by her with emotion.

Weight against weight; fluid with fluid; inside against, filled, packed with outside. He felt she was swallowing him, and he wanted to live inside her.

She shut her eyes, although she loved nothing more than to watch his face, over hers, under hers; and see him feeling what she is feeling. She can feel him brimming and flooding. She never imagined a man could feel as she did. She always wanted to lose her body in the throes of pleasure, to become pure sensation. But that, she knew, is not the way a man feels. A man never forgets his body the way a woman does, because a man is pushing his body, a part of his body, forward, to make the act of love happen. He brings the jut of his body into the act of love, then takes it back, when it has had its way. That was the way men were. But now she knew that a man could feel as she did, in his whole body. That a man could allow himself to groan and cling, just as she did when he mounted her and pierced her. That he wanted to be taken by her as much as she wanted to be taken by him. That she did not have to pretend to feel more pleasure than she did; that he yielded to her as much as she yielded to him. That they both embarked on the adventure of pleasure with the same slight anxiety about their ability to please or be pleased, and the same ease, the same trust. That they were equals in pleasure, because equals in love.

Meanwhile, the world is still out there: the inexhaustible mystery of simultaneity. While this is happening, that is also happening. Meanwhile, both Vesuvius and Etna flamed and smoked. The members of the trio prepared to drift off to sleep. The Cavaliere in his bed, thinking of his drowned treasures, of the volcano, of his lost world. And his beloved wife and beloved friend interlaced in another bed, thinking of each other in the fullness of satisfied desire. They kissed delicately. Sleep, my love. Sleep, she repeats to him. He says he cannot sleep, he is too happy. Talk to me, he said. I love your voice. She begins to muse astutely about the latest news from Naples: the slow effectiveness of Captain Troubridge's blockade, which had begun in late March; the surprising progress of Cardinal Ruffo's Christian army, now seventeen thousand strong; the difficulty of . . . He fell asleep while she was talking. The hero loves to sleep now.

Endless Love

Scott Spencer was born in Washington, D.C., grew up in Chicago, and graduated from the University of Wisconsin. He is the author of six critically acclaimed novels, Last Night at the Brown Thieves Ball, Preservational Hall, Endless Love, Waking the Dead, Secret Anniversaries, *and* Men in Black. *This excerpt is from* Endless Love, *a work of shatteringly powerful eroticism. He lives in Rhinebeck, New York, with his wife and children.*

WE HAD KISSED AND STROKED EACH OTHER FOR A WHILE. Jade straddled me and I thrust up to enter her, but missed. She took hold of me and guided me in. She felt a little dry and her discharge was thick, viscous—the result of her period, the blood mixed with her normal secretions. She winced as I entered her—it's awful, really, how stirring men find those small signs of pain. She lifted herself up a little, and I popped loose of her. She came back down until the knobby bones of our hips touched and the bow-shaped curve of my cock pressed into the cushy heart of her genitals, sinking until it hit a ridge of cartilage. I pressed her at the small of her back; her hips were locked around mine now and I felt her pubic hair brushing against me, as soft as breath on my belly. I pulled her down, made her bend from the waist and crushed our chests together.

I whispered her name and when she didn't respond I felt a moment's panic.

I held her face and kissed her mouth. Her tongue felt huge, soft, and unbearably alive in my mouth. I breathed her breath. It was the night's first real kiss. Precise, enormous.

She was up on her knees, her small breasts dangling a little, the light on the floor illuminating each strand of down. I put my hand between her thighs and cupped her vagina and Jade opened herself to me, posing for my fingers. She was open at her center and it was at least ten degrees warmer there.

Then, suddenly, I was inside her. I would have wanted to stop, to absorb the moment. She was straddling me, her hands on either side of my head, her forehead pressed against mine. She moved slowly, with her eyes screwed tightly shut, until I was all the way inside of her, and then she rocked back and forth, pressing herself against me with such huge power that I thought I might cry out. Yet it was not pain, of course — the intention of her pressure was specifically sexual and so potentially ecstatic that my nerve ends could only disregard their habits of response. The power with which she ground herself against me was awesome; it was all I really felt. I could sense the division in her genitals yet I could feel myself inside her only indistinctly.

To keep her balance, Jade planted the heel of her hand in a wedge of soft muscles beneath my shoulder. I felt surrounded by a membrane of pleasure, a huge, incandescent cocoon, brilliant and opaque for the most part but diaphanous at this curve or that. And through those patches of pleasure from which the color had somehow drained, I was intermittently aware of the shadows on the wall, the creak of the bedsprings, the peevish nuzzle of one prominent mattress button. Then, like a slowly revolving dome, the pleasure surrounded me in all of its opacity and I was lost again.

I was covered in sweat; my muscles ached as if knotted by fever. Someone somewhere in the hotel flushed a toilet and the sound roared through the thicket of my senses.

Jade moved back and forth, back and forth. I could tell she was not altogether with me. I'd never remembered, never thought of making love as something so *private*. The only commitment was one of need, but it seemed to stop there.

Jade kept one hand on me to hold her balance and placed her free hand on her belly. I noticed it dimly and wondered if she were in pain—a menstrual spasm, perhaps. But her hand slipped down, led by her extended index finger, and headed straight for her clitoris, lodging itself in that small space that existed between my pudendum and hers. She stroked herself with a rapid, circular motion while she raised and lowered herself on me. It seemed devastatingly expert of her. I could imagine it diagrammed in a book, explained at a symposium. Perhaps that sounds humorous, but it wasn't at the time. Her up and down motions were steady but incomplete: she had somehow calculated the degree of withdrawal

and repenetration that best accompanied her finger's masturbatory spiral.

She was even too expert to forget me. She fixed her eyes
on mine for a moment and then closed them, as if in a swoon.
She bent low to touch my face with her lips—so dry, as if she
were lost in a sexual desert and my face was only a mirage.
But she did kiss me, and when I captured her retreating mouth
with my own kiss she lingered, breathing the air out of my
lungs and exhaling into me the pungent blend of our combined redolence—the flat red wine, the long night, and the
radiation of our nervous systems.

The dome of pleasure my senses had crouched beneath was
no less opaque but it seemed to have risen: it no longer en-
veloped me like a blanket but now sheltered like a tent. I could
feel my own orgasm moving within me but it would suddenly
dart in some new direction, like a fish hiding within a coral
reef.

When her climax came—and it appeared suddenly, like in
accident—Jade trembled and made a high whinny, as if in
distress. Then she was absolutely still, like a startled animal
etched in the brightening beam of speeding headlights. Her
mouth was open; it seemed as if she might drool but she closed
her lips and lifted her chin, breathing out so heavily that her
belly swelled and made her look pregnant for a moment.

Of course when you love someone it is a tireless passion
to experience their pleasure, especially sexual pleasure. Of
all the many perversions, the one I found myself most capa-
ble of succumbing to was voyeurism—as long as the object
of my voyeurism was Jade. I never failed to be moved by her

expressions of sexual pleasure. When we were first learning to make love and I had some trouble in controlling myself, she had to be careful to keep as quiet as possible. Even heavy breathing would speed my climax, not to even mention moans. Later in our life together, when we were making love three, four, and five times a night (for our passion grew with our prowess), Jade would sometimes become impatient for my final orgasm—which would come with more difficulty than hers, because of the natural differences between the genders—and to bring us safely home so we both might fall asleep she would feign groans of pleasure with her lips right next to my ear, or say my name. It wouldn't really take anything more than that.

And so it was that night. As soon as her body began to jerk and shudder in response to her climax, I found myself astoundingly moved—as if by choral music that surprises you, or a kiss from behind bestowed by your lover on tiptoes. Jade let out her high keening call and I felt an abrupt rush of my semen, racing through me like twin rivers, turning with an acidic twist but not slowing down. I grabbed hold of her back, instinctually afraid she might leave me, and I arched myself toward her as I came. I could sense my pleasure passing through me almost unnoticed and I tried to fix my entire concentration on it. A perceptual lunge—like trying to discover the silver arc of a shooting star whose dive through the sky you've just caught out of the corner of your eye. When Jade felt the blurry warmth of my climax, she moved up a little and tightened herself for a slow, deliberate slide down. Whatever semen I had surrendered at the coaxing of Jade's fingers had left a prodigious storehouse behind—almost a *creepy* abundance. My scrotum, feet, hands went icy cold and my mouth—moments before filled with the slosh of desire—was dry as a wafer. My muscles were collapsing, my lungs shriveled like burst balloons, but I continued to come.

Sophie's Choice

William Styron's much publicized bout with depression has obscured momentarily the life-affirming character of the bulk of his output and the artistry of his fiction. The only (arguably) writer who can claim to be Faulkner's literary heir, he has continually found ways of surprising and enchanting his readers with sober and mature takes on important themes that would fold like old paper in the hands of a lesser talent. Slavery, the Holocaust, venereal disease—these are odd choices for a Virginian, but the works that deal with these themes are part of the modern canon, as well they should be. Sophie's Choice, a deep and intricate novel about a love affair between a woman who has survived Auschwitz and a young American writer, is still waiting its proper due, in spite of being made into a successful movie, being a bestseller, and winning critical acclaim.

I BEGAN TO KISS SOPHIE LIKE A MAN DYING OF THIRST AND she returned my kisses, groaning, but this is all we did (or all I could do, despite her gently expert, tickling manipulation) for many minutes. It would be misleading to emphasize my malfunction, either its duration or its effect on me, although such was its completeness that I recall resolving to commit suicide if it did not soon correct itself. Yet there it remained in her fingers, a limp worm. She slid down over the surface of my belly and began to suck me. I remember once how, in the abandonment of her confession regarding Nathan, she fondly spoke of him calling her "the world's most elegant cocksucker." He may have been right; I will never forget how eagerly and how naturally she moved to demonstrate to me her appetite and her devotion, planting her knees firmly between my legs like the fine craftswoman she was, then bending down and taking into her mouth my no longer quite so shrunken little comrade, bringing it swelling and jumping up by such a joyfully adroit, heedlessly noisy blend of labial and lingual rhythms that I could feel the whole slippery-sweet union of mouth and rigid prick like an electric charge running from my scalp to the tips of my toes. "Oh, Stingo," she gasped, pausing once for breath, "don't come yet, darling." Fat chance. I would lie there and let her suck me until my hair grew thin and gray.

The varieties of sexual experience are, I suppose, so multifarious that it is an exaggeration to say that Sophie and I did that night everything it is possible to do. But I'll swear we came close, and one thing forever imprinted on my brain was our mutual inexhaustibility. I was inexhaustible because I was twenty-two, and a virgin, and was clasping in my arms at last the goddess of my unending fantasies. Sophie's lust was as boundless as my own, I'm sure, but for more complex reasons;

it had to do, of course, with her good raw natural animal passion, but it was also both a plunge into carnal oblivion and a flight from memory and grief. More than that, I now see, it was a frantic and orgiastic attempt to beat back death. But at the time I was unable to perceive this, running as I was the temperature of an overheated Sherman tank, being out of my wits with excitement, and filled all night long with dumb wonder at our combined frenzy. For me it was less an initiation than a complete, well-rounded apprenticeship, or more, and Sophie, my loving instructress, never ceased whispering encouragement into my ear. It was as if through a living tableau, in which I myself was a participant, there were being acted out all the answers to the questions with which I had half maddened myself ever since I began secretly reading marriage manuals and sweated over the pages of Havelock Ellis and other sexual savants. Yes, the female nipples did spring up like little pink semihard gumdrops beneath the fingers, and Sophie emboldened me to even sweeter joys by asking me to excite them with my tongue. Yes, the clitoris was really there, darling little bud; Sophie placed my fingers on it. And oh, the cunt was indeed wet and warm, wet with a saliva-slick wetness that astounded me with its heat; the stiff prick slid in and out of that incandescent tunnel more effortlessly than I had ever dreamed, and when for the first time I spurted prodigiously somewhere in her dark bottomlessness, I heard Sophie cry out against my cheek, saying that she could feel the gush. The cunt also tasted good, I discovered later, as the church bell — no longer admonitory — dropped four gongs in the night; the cunt was simultaneously pungent and briny and I heard Sophie sigh, guiding me gently by the ears as if they were handles while I licked her there.

And then there were all those famous positions. Not the twenty-eight outlined in the handbooks, but certainly, in addition to the standard one, three or four or five. At some point Sophie, returning from the bathroom where she kept the liquor, switched on the light, and we fucked in a glow of soft copper; I was delighted to find that the "female superior" posture was every bit as pleasurable as Dr. Ellis had claimed, not so much for its anatomical advantages (though those too were fine, I thought as from below I cupped Sophie's breasts in my hands or, alternately, squeezed and stroked her bottom) as for the view it afforded me of that wide-boned Slavic face brooding above me, her eyes closed and her expression so beautifully tender and drowned and abandoned in her passion that I had to avert my gaze. "I can't stop coming," I heard her murmur, and I knew she meant it. We lay quietly together for a while, side by side, but soon without a word Sophie presented herself in such a way as to fulfill all my past fantasies in utter apotheosis. Taking her from behind while she knelt, thrusting into the cleft between those smooth white globes, I suddenly clenched my eyes shut and, I remember, thought in a weird seizure of cognition of the necessity of redefining "joy," "fulfillment," "ecstasy," even "God." Several times we stopped long enough for Sophie to drink, and for her to pour whiskey and water down my own gullet. The booze, far from numbing me, heightened the images as well as the sensations of what then bloomed into phantasmagoria . . . Her voice in my ear, the incomprehensible words in Polish nonetheless understood, urging me on as if in a race, urging me to some ever-receding finish line. Fucking for some reason on the gritty bone-hard floor, the reason unclear, dim, stupid—*why*, for Christ's sake?—then abruptly dawning: to view, as on a pornographic screen, our pale white entwined bodies splashing back from the lusterless mirror on the bathroom door. A kind of furious obsessed wordlessness finally—no Polish, no English, no language, only breath. *Soixante-neuf* (recommended by the doctor), where after smothering for minute after minute in her moist mossy cunt's undulant swamp, I came at last in Sophie's mouth, came in a spasm of such delayed, prolonged, exquisite intensity that I verged on a scream, or a prayer, and my vision went blank, and I gratefully perished. Sleep then—a sleep that was beyond mere sleep. Cold-cocked. Etherized. Dead.

Museum Pieces

Elizabeth Tallent is the author of three short-story collections, In Constant Flight, Time with Children, *and* Honey, *as well as a novel,* Museum Pieces, *and a critical work,* Married Men and Magic Tricks: John Updike's Erotic Heroes. *Her work is noteworthy for its intellectual clarity, deep emotional sympathy, and icily elegant precision. This excerpt is from* Museum Pieces.

PETER AND MIA ARE ASLEEP IN HER BEDROOM, HER KNEE tucked between his legs, his hand caught in her hair, so that when he moves in his dream, the jerk at the nape of her neck draws her awake. His baseball shirt is draped across the back of a chair, his jacket crumpled on the floor, one of his running shoes is in a corner. Pancho Villa sleeps at the foot of the bed, his nose tucked beneath one paw.

She turns in the tangled sheets and studies Peter. Peter is the first man whose body has ever seemed entirely right to her. He makes her aware, in retrospect, of how clumsy she sometimes was with Cody, freezing, she had hoped imperceptibly, before he entered her, her knees drawing up as if she needed some measure of protection from him. With Cody, she had closed her eyes, though he had wanted her to keep them open. With Peter things are disconcertingly opposite. Before he comes he nudges her face away, his chin scraping her jaw, as if he loves her best in slightly submissive profile — as if he were the one who needed protection. In the darkness of the rumpled bed she admires his feet, the long slanting muscles of his thighs, the wreath of wiry hairs around the flat brown nipples. She slides downward in the bed, pushing at Pancho Villa's sly, settled weight with her foot. It is still spring and the cat has already caught two sparrows and one swallowtail butterfly that lived for a while after he brought it into the house — an attempt, she knew, to regain the place in her affections that has been usurped by Peter.

She strokes one of his thighs, the cowlick of coarser hair near the scrotum, which dips down elegantly, as if to counterbalance the shaft of the penis, slowly becoming erect. When he walked toward her naked for the first time in the basement, his penis bobbled and he caught it shyly in his hand and hid it. She loved that. Now with half-shut eyes she touches her tongue to the hood whose texture is slightly grainy, not nearly as smooth as it looks; she runs her tongue into the downy cleft, a little urgingly, to see if the first teardrop will bead the cleft, but it doesn't. She tastes the faint salt bitterness of urine and a waxy trace of Ivory soap. Above her, far above, he says her name. She rests her teeth, just the very edges of her front teeth, on the skin of the penis. Her tongue rises to the ridge of vein on the shaft, smooth as a peeled twig, ample with the blood inside that makes the vein blue or sometimes gray; if he is sufficiently aroused she can sometimes see a quickening and tightening of that vein. Farther down there are his balls and a different taste, richer and somewhat sour—she thinks of the venison Cody fed her a bite of, once, when a friend of his had shot a buck. The hair there is kinky, unlike the hair anywhere else on his body. She slips one of the balls into her mouth and the lucid floating egg shape rests on her tongue inside its pouch of coarse, pliant skin. She pushes it out very gently with her tongue and sucks on the other ball and then she rises and takes the end of the penis into her mouth, deeply, down to the scallops on either side of the hood, and she remembers being very small and scared in summer camp when someone had made her put a flashlight into her mouth and turn it on, so that the glare of the light through skin was tinted red, a monster's grimace, or a ghost's; there was, then, this metallic sliding smoothness and a feeling of helplessness. She stops, and he slips from her mouth, his penis flipping up against his belly with a soft clap. He moves down at the same instant that she moves upward, and he turns so that he is above her, and she can feel his ribs looming between her knees and she rubs her callused heels against his back to make the pleasing sandpaper friction. He says her name. It doesn't sound like her name. He says, "Clarissa."

The Paper Anniversary

Joan Wickersham is a novelist and short story writer. This selection is from her debut novel, The Paper Anniversary, *which has been called "a modern comedy of errors." Her writing is characterized by warmth, tenderness, and an intelligent blending of sharp insights and wry humor.*

THEN THEY WERE SILENT, AND THEY MUST HAVE FALLEN asleep. He woke up some time later to feel the radiator's steel ribs mashed against his back, his legs sticking out stiffly in front of him. The clock at the back of Maisie's old stove said quarter to four. She was asleep on top of the covers, her glasses still on her face but askew, one stem down along her cheek and nearly touching her mouth. He moved on his knees over to the bed, and gently he took her glasses off, folded them, and set them on the stool that served as her bedside table. Her nightgown was draped smoothly over her knees, and her small feet were crossed at the ankles, as though she were a tomb effigy. He'd forgotten how neatly she slept. Even her breathing was pretty: soft little exhalations of the lips and nostrils, hushed and controlled, like the sounds she'd made when she smoked. Her eyelids were shiny and faintly pink, trembling with whatever dreams went on beneath them. He put a hand on her face, his fingertips tracing the cheekbone, and without increasing the pressure of that hand, he used the other arm to push himself up onto the bed beside her. There was hardly any room, and he lay on his side with his left arm beneath him, the right hand still resting lightly on her face.

"Unnnh," she said softly, and then she opened her eyes and looked at him.

He turned away, reached up over their heads and switched off the light. He began to kiss her, gently at first, but then harder: she'd got him after all. But he didn't want to think, he wanted her nightgown off, her knees open, her arms stretched over her head. And after a while he felt her shaking beneath him and knew that she was coming, or crying; he didn't care which.

Acknowledgments

From "Kathy Goes to Haiti" included in *Literal Madness* by Kathy Acker. Copyright © 1978 by Kathy Acker. Used by permission of Grove/Atlantic, Inc.

From *The Adventures of Augie March* by Saul Bellow. Copyright © 1949, 1951, 1952, 1953 by Saul Bellow. Used by permission of Viking Penguin, a division of Penguin Books USA, Inc.

From *Come to Me* by Amy Bloom. Copyright © 1993 by Amy Bloom. Reprinted by permission of HarperCollins Publishers, Inc.

From *The Geography of Desire* by Robert Boswell. Copyright © 1989 by Robert Boswell. Reprinted by permission of Alfred A. Knopf, Inc.

From *Stories in an Almost Classical Mode* by Harold Brodkey. Copyright © 1988 by Harold Brodkey. Reprinted by permission of Alfred A. Knopf, Inc.

From *Harry and Catherine* by Frederick Busch. Copyright © 1991 by Frederick Busch. Reprinted by permission of Alfred A. Knopf, Inc.

From *They Whisper* by Robert Olen Butler. Copyright © 1994 by Robert Olen Butler. Reprinted by permission of Henry Holt & Co., Inc.

From *Melting Point* by Pat Califia. Copyright © 1993 Pat Califia. Reprinted by permission of Alyson Publications, Inc.

Reprinted with permission of Scribner, a division of Simon & Schuster, from *The Star Cafe and Other Stories* by Mary Caponegro. Copyright © 1990 by Mary Caponegro.

From *The Mysteries of Pittsburgh* by Michael Chabon. Copyright © 1998 by Michael Chabon. Reprinted by permission of William Morrow & Company, Inc.

From *The Point* by Charles D'Ambrosio. Copyright © 1995 by Charles D'Ambrosio. By permission of Little, Brown and Company.

From *Players* by Don DeLillo. Copyright © 1977 by Don DeLillo. Reprinted by permission of Alfred A. Knopf, Inc.

From *Billy Bathgate* by E. L. Doctorow. Copyright © 1989 by E. L. Doctorow. Reprinted by permission of Random House, Inc.

From *All Set About with Fever Trees* by Pam Durban. Copyright © 1985, 1995 by Pam Durban. Reprinted by permission of Brandt & Brandt Literary Agents, Inc.

From *The Invisible Circus* by Jennifer Egan. Copyright © 1995 by Jennifer Egan. Used by permission of Doubleday, a division of Bantam Doubleday Dell Publishing Group, Inc.

From *ARC d'X* by Steve Erickson. Copyright © 1993 by Steve Erickson. Reprinted by permission of Melanie Jackson Agency, L.L.C.

From *Nude Men* by Amanda Filipacchi. Copyright © 1993 by Amanda Filipacchi. Used by permission of Viking Penguin, a division of Penguin Books USA, Inc.

From *Family Night* by Maria Flook. Copyright © 1993 by Maria Flook. Reprinted by permission of Pantheon Books, a division of Random House, Inc.

Reprinted with the permission of Simon & Schuster from *Because They Wanted To* by Mary Gaitskill. Copyright © 1997 by Mary Gaitskill.

From *The Mind-Body Problem* by Rebecca Goldstein. Copyright © 1983 by Rebecca Goldstein. Originally published by Random House. Reprinted with permission of author.

Acknowledgments

From *The Ring of Brightest Angels Around Heaven* by Rick Moody. Copyright © 1995 by Rick Moody. By permission of Little, Brown and Company.

From *The Whiteness of Bones* by Susanna Moore. Copyright © 1959 by Susanna Moore. Used by permission of Doubleday, a division of Bantam Doubleday Dell Publishing Group, Inc.

From *Jazz* by Toni Morrison. Copyright © 1992 by Alfred A. Knopf, Inc. Reprinted by permission of International Creative Management, Inc.

From *Last Days* by Joyce Carol Oates. Copyright © 1984 by The Ontario Review, Inc. Used by permission of Dutton Signet, a division of Penguin Books USA, Inc.

Excerpt from *These Same Long Bones* by Gwendolyn Parker. Copyright © 1994 by Gwendolyn Parker. Reprinted by permission of Houghton Mifflin Company. All rights reserved.

Excerpt from *Martin and John* by Dale Peck. Copyright © 1993 by Dale Peck. Reprinted by permission of Farrar, Straus & Giroux, Inc.

Excerpt from *The Professor of Desire* by Philip Roth. Copyright © 1977 by Philip Roth. Reprinted by permission of Farrar, Straus & Giroux, Inc.

From *Acquainted with the Night* by Lynne Sharon Schwartz. Copyright © 1984 by Lynne Sharon Schwartz. Reprinted by permission of International Creative Management, Inc.

From *Playing with Fire* by Dani Shapiro. Copyright © 1990 Dani Shapiro. Used by permission of Doubleday, a division of Bantam Doubleday Dell Publishing Group, Inc.

From *Touch* by Charlotte Watson Sherman. Copyright © 1995 by Charlotte Watson Sherman. Reprinted by permission of HarperCollins Publishers, Inc.

From *A Thousand Acres* by Jane Smiley. Copyright © 1991 by Jane Smiley. Reprinted by permission of Alfred A. Knopf, Inc.

Acknowledgments

Excerpt from *The Volcano Lover* by Susan Sontag. Copyright ©
1992 by Susan Sontag. Reprinted by permission of Farrar,
Straus & Giroux, Inc.

From *Endless Love* by Scott Spencer. Copyright © 1991 by Scott
Spencer. Reprinted by permission of Alfred A. Knopf, Inc.

From *Sophie's Choice* by William Styron. Copyright © 1976,
1978, 1979 by William Styron. Reprinted by permission of Random House, Inc.

From *Museum Pieces* by Elizabeth Tallent. Copyright © 1985
by Elizabeth Tallent. Reprinted by permission of Alfred A.
Knopf, Inc.

From *The Paper Anniversary* by Joan Wickersham. Copyright ©
1993 by Joan Wickersham. Used by permission of Viking Penguin, a division of Penguin Books USA, Inc.